PAP/018

# BONES OF THE
# BUFFALO

# BONES OF THE BUFFALO

## LEWIS B. PATTEN

**Thorndike Press** • **Chivers Press**
**Thorndike, Maine USA** **Bath, England**

This Large Print edition is published by Thorndike Press, USA
and by Chivers Press, England.

Published in 2000 in the U.S. by arrangement with
Golden West Literary Agency.

Published in 2000 in the U.K. by arrangement with
Golden West Literary Agency.

U.S.  Hardcover  0-7862-2275-1  (Western Series Edition)
U.K.  Hardcover  0-7540-4023-2  (Chivers Large Print)
U.K.  Softcover   0-7540-4024-0  (Camden Large Print)

The text of this Large Print edition is unabridged.
Other aspects of the book may vary from the original edition.

Set in 16 pt. Plantin by Al Chase.

Printed in the United States on permanent paper.

**British Library Cataloguing-in-Publication Data available**

**Library of Congress Cataloging-in-Publication Data**
Patten, Lewis B.
    Bones of the buffalo / Lewis B. Patten.
        p.    cm.
    ISBN 0-7862-2275-1  (lg. print : hc : alk. paper)
    1. Cheyenne Indians — Fiction.   2. Large type books.
I. Title.
PS3566.A79 B59 2000
813'.54—dc21                                                99-049184

Once proud and defiant, the Cheyenne were now broken by the white man's relentless westward push. They had finally been forced southward to a reservation far from their homelands. Though unhappy, the tribes tried to adjust to their new way of life . . . until the continual mistreatment and broken promises of the Indian agents led to starvation and sickness. In desperation, a band of three hundred valiant Cheyenne, mostly women and children, slipped away to begin a long journey back home. It was the start of one of the most heroic marches in history — and also of a bitter struggle that swept through the Northwest territory for more than three months.

# CHAPTER ONE

It lay in a shallow bowl, hidden from the eyes of the world, a place of death that still smelled of death. The bones were scattered now, scattered by wolves and coyotes tearing the rotting flesh from them, but here and there a whole carcass remained intact, the rib cage looking almost as huge as the wagon bows of a Conestoga.

The grass was greener here because of the fertilizing of running blood and rotting flesh and the dung of the scavengers. And the sky was blue today, dotted with puffy, drifting clouds that had broken off from the huge pile to the southeast, hanging solid over the Sappa twenty miles away.

Orvie Watts drew his six mules to a halt at the top of the ridge and stared at the more than five acres of bleaching bones from which the blackened shreds of flesh still hung. Behind him, his aging, tongueless helper John halted the other wagon and looked at him expectantly. Orvie spoke in a voice cracked from lack of use. "Somebody sure as hell had hisself a stand here, by God. Must be two hundred head, at least."

John made a sound that was formless and just a sound, but Orvie knew it was agreement with his words. He said, "Let's get loaded, then, and tomorrow morning we'll head back for Dodge."

John made another sound at his mules, a wordless shout, and slapped their backs with the reins. They moved ahead, around the wagon of Orvie Watts and out into the valley of bleaching bones, crunching the loose ones lying scattered around beneath their hoofs and the wagon's huge, iron-tired wheels. John halted them and climbed stiffly down after tying the reins and setting the wagon's brake.

Orvie sat for a moment on his wagon's seat, staring, a light frown on his seamed, gray-whiskered face. He was a wiry, middle-aged, practical man not given to dreams or thoughtfulness, but something about this place brought memories drifting back to his mind out of the vast emptiness of the past. The bones of the buffalo lying before him came to life and stood with shaggy heads raised, nostrils flaring into the wind and black hoofs pawing ferociously, raising clouds of dust that drifted slowly away across the rest of the nervously shifting herd.

His eyes took on a look that was almost

the look of dreaming, and he saw once more a plain stretching away as far as the eye could reach and blackened with buffalo for all that distance and more. He saw the half naked, bronzed bodies of the Indian hunters galloping and he saw the conical hide tipis with flaps spread at their tops to draw up the smoke from the fires below. And he saw the smooth face of an Indian girl, the eyes so dark and liquid and filled with love . . . His face twisted suddenly with an ugly kind of pain, ugly because it was the pain of guilt, and he shouted harshly at his teams. With bones crunching beneath the wagon's wheels, he pulled ahead across the natural bowl and stopped where the bones were thick around him, white and stinking and valuable, though not as valuable as the buffalo hides had been.

He got down after setting his brake and began to load the wagon bed that already held nearly half a load gathered elsewhere on the plain. He worked with a single-minded concentration that was almost anger, hating the black bugs that scurried away from everything he moved which had previously covered the ground.

Some of the bits of curly brown hair and hide still clung to the buffalo heads, but they had been dry too long to harbor maggots any more. The horns and the brown, curly hair and the empty eye sockets had a way of seeming real to him, the eye sockets staring as though blaming him for what had happened here, for what had happened in a thousand other places all across the great, high plains.

So he worked, angrily and sometimes almost frantically, until his body was soaked with acrid-smelling sweat that ran off his forehead and into his eyes, until he was breathing as hard as if he had been running away . . .

And indeed he had. Running away from his memories. Running away because there had been beauty in the past, because there was only ugliness here, and death.

This smell . . . this sweetish, sickish smell of death had been in his nostrils so long he would have missed it if it had gone. He had hunted the buffalo when they ran thick and black as a tide across these grassy plains, and he had hunted them when they thinned to a small sprinkling in the shallow, hidden draws, and he had hunted them when they moved north, and south, and he had even hunted them below the Arkansas where hunting them was forbidden by the law.

And when there were not enough left so that a man could live by hunting them, he had joined many another buffalo hunter and had become a bone picker, a scavenger, a gatherer-up of the refuse of the hunt.

Death had become a way of life with him a long, long time ago, and he had known he was killing more than the buffalo. He had helped kill the Indian, who lived on the buffalo, but he had done something worse, even than that. He had helped kill a way of life, a free, open, unfettered way of life that he once had loved and still remembered.

Knowing it, he had not stopped but had gone on killing because the death of that way of life was inevitable and unavoidable, and because in his own pain he had wanted to hasten its dying struggle and bring his torment to an end.

Ahead of him John, the mute, worked in silence except for the soft, almost animal grunting sounds he made each time he stooped. The bones clattered into the wagons and their beds began to fill. The sun slid from its zenith down the cloud-spotted sky toward the horizon in Colorado to the west. Orvie stopped to catch his breath. His glance wandered downcountry toward the valley of the Sappa twenty miles away.

It was over now, and the good, free way of life was forever gone. The Cheyenne, both northern and southern, were captives on the reservation in Indian territory to the south. Beaten and sullen, they sat wrapped in their blankets dreaming of the glories of the past.

He wiped the sweat from his streaming forehead with the grimy back of a hand. He wondered what it was about this place that brought the past crowding back so vividly. He cursed softly beneath his breath.

The mules' heads lifted, and turned, pointing toward a rider that had just topped the shallow ridge to the south and west. Watts stared, wiping his palms on the sides of his trouser legs as if in anticipation of a handshake with the approaching man. Squinting slightly against the sun, he waited patiently.

The newcomer wore the blue of the U.S. Cavalry, with the yellow-striped trousers of a non-com. Reaching John, he started to speak, but stopped when John grinned at him and made an incoherent sound in his throat. John gestured toward Orvie and, somewhat disconcerted, the cavalryman came on to halt a second time beside Orvie's mules.

"Howdy."

Orvie nodded in reply.

"Looks like you're about to get loaded and go on in."

"Uh huh."

"Where do you take this stuff? To Dodge?"

Orvie nodded.

"What the hell do they use it for?"

"They grind it up and use it for fertilizer."

"Don't they use manure no more?"

"Sure. Only they use bones too."

The cavalryman turned his head and stared in awe at the litter of bones. "Dozen wagonloads here, looks like. Pay good, does it?"

"Not like hides." The cavalryman had not offered to dismount and shake hands so Orvie held himself aloof and a bit withdrawn. Some men just didn't have the stomach for this stink and he really couldn't blame them, he supposed. It was a thing a man had to get used to.

The Cavalryman seemed anxious to be on his way. He said, "I'm part of a troop warning settlers. Little Wolf and Dull Knife have broken loose from Fort Reno. They're headed up this way."

Orvie nodded, mildly surprised at the Cheyenne stubbornness but unworried. He'd be long gone before the Indians got this far, if indeed they did. The silence between them grew awkward and strained, neither of them having anything more to say. At last the trooper, a big, grizzled vet-

13

eran said, "Good luck, then."

"Yeah."

The trooper touched his horse's sides with his spurs and the animal moved away, untroubled by the bones or smell of death. The trooper topped the ridge to the north and disappeared.

Orvie went back to loading bones.

At sundown, the trooper struck a small stream running south-east toward the Sappa. There were the tracks of cattle along the banks of the narrow trickle, and the tracks of an unshod horse, fresh and made today.

Smiling faintly to himself in anticipation of a home-cooked meal and perhaps even a real bed, he touched spurs to his weary horse's sides and lifted him to a slow and rocking lope. The valley, narrow where he had first struck the stream, widened out as he traveled south, until at last it was three quarters of a mile wide and almost flat.

He came to a fence and rode along it to the stream where he found a wire gate. Dismounting, he opened it and led his horse through, afterward closing it again.

He was in a large hay meadow now, with stacks scattered across it like fat brown loaves of bread. And in the distance, in the growing dusk, he could see the buildings of a ranch.

The house was frame, once white but now weathered and needing paint. The roof, of cedar shakes, was gray with weathering, and here and there a missing shingle had been patched with a straightened out tin can which had subsequently rusted red. A two-story house, it stood gaunt and bleak against the darkening eastern sky, no lamps yet winking from its windows.

Not far from the back door of the house there was another building, this one built of sod, and roofed with sod, out of which grew weeds and grass three feet tall. This was the original dwelling here, probably now used for a root cellar.

Beyond the sod shack stood a barn, of un-planed, unpainted lumber that the weather had turned almost as gray as the roof of the house. And behind the barn was a corral, with a windmill nearby that discharged a stream of water into a pond half in and half outside of the corral. In the corral were two horses and, coming in toward the barn from the south was a milch cow and a calf, driven by a tow-headed boy the trooper judged to be about thirteen.

He drew in his horse beside the back door of the house, waited a moment expectantly, then called out, "Hello! Anybody home?"

The door opened and a woman came out onto the stoop and stood peering up at him. Behind her he could see the faces of two little girls, the oldest ten or eleven, he supposed, the youngest seven or eight. He had three little girls himself and so was fairly accurate in his judgments of their age.

He touched his hatbrim and waited for an invitation to dismount. The woman said, "What's a trooper doin' way out here?"

He felt her animosity pushing at him and his hopes of a home-cooked meal and bed began to fade. He said, swinging down off his horse unbidden as he spoke, "Dull Knife and Little Wolf have broken loose at Fort Reno, ma'am. If they ain't caught, they'll probably come this way like the Cheyenne did a couple of years ago. I'm part of a troop warning settlers."

She did not reply, but no concern touched her face. Fort Reno was a long ways off and she probably didn't even consider the possibility that the Cheyenne would get this far north before being caught. The trooper didn't think it likely either. He was just doing a job.

He heard a sound behind him. Turning his head, he saw a man approaching from the barn.

16

The man was of medium height, thickset and dark from exposure to the elements. His hair, curling uncut on his neck and above his ears, was yellow as straw, contrasting sharply with his deep-bronzed skin. He had a couple of days' yellow stubble on his jaws. His expression was almost grim, his blue eyes cold, yet in spite of this the trooper felt a strange, instantaneous liking for the man.

The man stuck out his hand. "Howdy, trooper. I'm Morgan Cross. What brings you 'way out here?"

The trooper repeated what he had told Cross's wife. He saw the way Cross's glance went briefly to his wife. He did not miss the coldness that had intensified itself in Cross's eyes.

Cross said, "What's the Army expect us to do, pick up our stuff and move out until they're caught?"

The trooper shrugged. "Just be on guard. Maybe keep your doors locked and a gun handy. I guess that's all."

"Well, thanks for warning us." Cross turned his head and peered at his wife standing before the door. "You ask this man to stay the night?"

She shook her head.

Cross said, "Stay the night with us,

trooper, unless you have to get back to wherever your troop is camped."

"It'll be a pleasure, Mr. Cross." But he wasn't sure it would. He could sense the animosity between this husband and his wife. A coldness like the winter air that the sun's warmth cannot thaw.

He wondered at it and at its cause. He envied men who were able to spend each day and night with their families. The woman backed away into the kitchen and lighted a lamp. Cross opened and held the door for the trooper, who went inside and stood, hat in hand, in the middle of the warm kitchen while the two little girls giggled in the doorway to the dining room. He said, "I'm Corporal Delaney, Mr. Cross."

Cross nodded, said, "Glad to know you, Corporal," and went on into the dining room. He lighted a lamp and carried it into a parlor beyond. Delaney followed him. There was a leather-covered sofa and a leather-covered chair. The corporal sat in the chair and Cross sank down on the sofa. The two little girls stood in the doorway staring at the corporal until their father said, "You two scat."

Neither of them left and they continued to giggle. Their father grinned affectionately at them.

He looked at the corporal. "You see the Murphys on Cut-Nose Creek west of here?"

The trooper shook his head. "But I ran into a couple of bone pickers in a little hollow about half a dozen miles southwest."

Cross's grin faded. His eyes grew angry suddenly. The trooper asked, "They trespassin' on your land?"

Cross glanced at him and shook his head. "Not trespassing, I guess. I don't own that land." He grinned with faint self-mockery. "I guess I just hate to see things changed. Sometimes I ride up there and look at all those bones and remember what it was like when there were live buffalo grazing there."

The back door slammed and Delaney heard the clatter of milk pails and a boy's changing voice. Cross called, "Take care of the trooper's horse, Jess, on your way out to milk."

"Sure Pa." The back door slammed again.

# CHAPTER TWO

When it was ready, Nellie Cross called her husband and the trooper for supper, her voice neutral and without emotion of any kind. The two came into the kitchen and seemed to fill it when they did despite its size. The children, already washed, sat at the table staring at the trooper's broad, dusty back. There was a smell to him, of sweat and horse and saddle leather that was by no means an unpleasant one.

While her husband's back was turned, Nellie watched him and tonight her expression twisted faintly with something that might almost have been physical pain. Strain was constant between them now, she thought. He was home only when he had to be, for food, or sleep, and even those two necessities were found elsewhere whenever it was possible.

It was her fault. It was her fault and she could end it whenever she chose. Even now, after seven years. She could end it but she knew she would not. Because if she did, she would die. It would kill her to bear another child. She knew that as surely as she had ever known anything. The last one had nearly killed her seven years ago.

She served the food without looking directly at her husband's face, but very conscious of him just the same. Nor did he look at her. But the trooper did, his face wearing an expression of puzzlement.

Having served the food, she sat down silently, filled her plate and began to eat. How long could two people live this way? she wondered. How long, with coldness like ice between them despite the surface courtesy they showed each other for the children's sake? Maybe it would be better if they fought. That, at least, would show feeling. It would show they cared.

Sometimes she hated herself for her own cowardice. A man as virile and strong as Morgan deserved something better than a wife who was too cowardly to be a wife.

A couple of times a year it got to be more than he could stand. When it did he would mumble something to her about needing supplies and would ride to Julesburg over in Colorado more than a hundred miles away. He would be gone a week and would return with red bloodshot eyes and a look of shame about his face. Gradually the shame would change to defiant anger, and not long after that the old coldness would reappear.

She knew what he did when he went to Julesburg and the knowledge was like a knife twisting in her heart. But she had no right to feel that way. If she had been what she should have been to him the trips would have been unnecessary.

Morgan Cross was up before dawn, as he always was, and out in the kitchen with a fire going in the stove before the eastern horizon turned gray. This morning, though, he did not stay but went out and saddled a horse for himself. He rode away without breakfast, before anyone else was up.

# CHAPTER THREE

Not particularly anxious to return home, Morgan turned his horse and rode south toward the Sappa. The miles dropped slowly away behind. He recalled his talks with the trooper and that made him think about the Cheyenne.

He had nothing particular against Indians. He did not resent them or blame them for their attempts to hold their land. But neither did he feel that he had taken land from them. So far as he knew, Indians had never camped upon the land he held or used. He'd had nothing to do with killing off their game, any more than his father had.

A score of times since his family had been here on this land, Indians had stopped at the Cross ranch house. All those times but one, they had been peaceable, though they sometimes used thinly veiled threats to get what they wanted — usually food. A couple of times they had wanted horses and both times Morgan's father had given them horses to avoid trouble with them. But once they had wanted scalps. Morgan and his father and mother had fought them off from the sod shack for two days before a party of buffalo hunters heard the shots and intervened.

Now the Indians were gone. The last of them, the northern Cheyenne, had been hauled south to Indian Territory a year ago. And even if they had broken out, even if they had started north, there was no longer any danger from them. They were too few and too poorly armed. If what Morgan had heard was true, they were half-starved as well.

Furthermore, there were settlers all over the great plains now. Three railroads cut across from east to west. The Indians could be intercepted and turned back easily.

Coming around a bend in the creek, he suddenly saw a mounted trooper ahead of him. Not the trooper who had spent the night at the ranch. Not an enlisted man. This man was an officer.

Cross approached, realizing that this was the exact spot on which the Henely massacre had taken place three years before. He could still see the piled-up, blackened remains of the burned tipis. In front of them he saw a bleaching human skull, a small skull, like that of a child.

Reaching the trooper, a lieutenant, he stopped, nodded, and leaned toward the man to extend his hand. "I'm Morgan Cross, Lieutenant. I guess you're part of the detachment that's out warning settlers."

The trooper took his hand, gripped it hard and let it go. He said, his voice deep and regular, "Yes sir. I'm Lieutenant Robert Mannion. My men are supposed to rendezvous here tonight."

Cross turned in his saddle and got two cigars out of his saddlebag. He gave one to the lieutenant and lighted the other himself. They were black and strong, but he puffed with real pleasure. The lieutenant, obviously used to a milder brand, licked his lips as though the smoke bit his tongue.

Mannion dismounted and Cross followed suit. He was not far from the skull and he noted that the top of it was smashed, either by a bullet or a rifle butt.

The lieutenant was also staring at the skull and at the remains of the fire beyond it. He said, "That was a helluva thing — what happened here three years ago. You'd think we'd learn eventually to treat Indians with a little humanity."

Cross said shortly, "They asked for it. They murdered the Germaine family and kidnapped the Germaine girls. People out here get stirred up when their women are staked out for a bunch of dirty Indian braves."

Lieutenant Mannion studied his face a moment, then bent and picked up the skull. "This one couldn't have been more than ten. Do you suppose he killed or raped anyone?"

Morgan glanced quickly at him. "That's kind of funny talk, coming from an Army man. That's our job out here — or was — keeping the Indians peaceable."

Mannion smiled. There was a hint of apology in his face and voice but Cross realized it was not apology for his views, only for so bluntly expressing them. He said, "You're right, of course. I just happen to think that feeding them would be a better means, and cheaper, of keeping them peaceful then shooting them." He grinned wryly. "Not everyone shares my views."

Cross peered closely at him. "Is food why Dull Knife and Little Wolf broke out?"

Mannion nodded. "That and disease and the fact that they were promised they could return to the Yellowstone if they didn't like it in the south."

"How many broke out, anyway?"

"Three hundred maybe. Men, women, and kids."

"Mounted and armed?"

The lieutenant shook his head. "No. A few had horses, and they'll steal more as they go. But not many of them had guns. And they had practically no food at all."

Cross frowned. It had suddenly occurred to him how strange it was that settlers were being warned this far north. Unless the Army feared the Cheyenne might fight their way on through. He asked, "When did they break out?"

"September ninth. Two weeks ago."

Cross's glance sharpened. "And where are they now?"

Mannion stared at his feet. "Nearly to the Arkansas, last I heard. They could be this side of it by now."

For a moment Cross was silent. Then he asked irritably, "And where the hell is the Army that's supposed to turn them back? Will you tell me that?"

Mannion shrugged and said evasively, "I suppose the Army is pursuing them."

Cross began to pace back and forth. He glanced across the creek toward the south uneasily. "You suppose! Well by God, that's fine! Here we sit, with three hundred Indians less'n a week away. Your trooper didn't say how close they were. You know what'll happen when they reach this place? They'll count up all the Cheyenne Henely killed here three years ago and they'll try to get themselves a white for every one. Do you know there wasn't a prisoner taken here?"

"I know."

"Well, dammit, what's the army going to do? Are they sending in more troops? Or are they snarled up in red tape the way they usually are?"

Mannion met his glance patiently. "I don't know what the Army plans to do. I just know what they have ordered me to do. That's to warn the settlers in this area and then move south and make contact with the troops that are pursuing the Indians."

"Well, I sure as hell know what I'm going to do! I'm going to get some men together! If the Army won't turn the Indians back, then by God we will!"

"Civilian action will only make things worse. I'd advise you, Mr. Cross . . ."

"Advise and be damned! Let me tell you something, Lieutenant. Two years ago, Lieutenant Henely and that bunch of buffalo hunters stopped these Indians . . ." He waved toward the blackened remains of the fire and went on. ". . . just twenty miles short of my ranch house."

Mannion interrupted, "Short? They were camped here, Mr. Cross."

"All right. They were camped here. But do you think they'd have stayed? They'd have moved north with the first pressure that was put on them. They'd have stripped my ranch of horses and cattle and they might have decided to burn the buildings too."

"You can't be sure. They were peaceful when Henely attacked them. They showed a flag of truce."

Cross shrugged. "Maybe. I don't know about that. What I do know is how people out here . . . civilians . . . feel about the Indians. Most of us have fought 'em a time or two. There's damn few of us that hasn't lost some member of his family to them."

Mannion, whose face had grown slightly red, now said placatingly, "I know, Mr. Cross. I know how you feel. I . . ."

"The hell you do!" Cross interrupted angrily.

Mannion's face turned a deeper red. His eyes snapped but he didn't speak.

Cross glared at him, feeling his own irritation begin to rise. He forced himself to smile but it was a thin smile. "I don't want to argue with you, Lieutenant. Besides, I think I'd better ride. I'm going to get some men together in case those Cheyenne get through."

The lieutenant returned his smile grudgingly and stuck out his hand again. "Goodbye, Mr. Cross."

Cross took the hand, gripped it perfunctorily, then mounted. He whirled his horse and touched spurs to his sides. He rode away galloping, in the direction of Cut-Nose Creek.

Mannion watched him go, his expression half-irritated, half-amused. He had liked Cross instantaneously, and he puzzled for a moment at the chemistry that sometimes draws men to each other this way. In Cross, he suspected, he would find a kindred soul, a man much like himself, in spite of their differing views.

# CHAPTER FOUR

The train puffed steadily through the warm September night. Ben Terborg sat at the window, staring moodily through its reflected images of things inside the car at the blackness outside of it. The window was clouded and dirty, but in spite of that he could see the fires on the south bank of the Arkansas, fires that winked in the night, illuminating sometimes the sleeping forms of troopers, or officers' tents, or a picket line of tethered cavalry mounts.

He glanced up as the conductor entered the car. The man said, "Army bivouac ahead and on the left, sir. Do you want to stop?"

Terborg nodded. He stared at the conductor a moment, then asked, "Can you signal them?"

The man nodded. "With the whistle, sir. I can get one of their officers over here, if that's what you mean."

Terborg nodded. "That's what I mean." He waited until the conductor had gone, then got up and blew out all the lamps that were burning to illuminate the inside of the car. He returned to the window and scrubbed at its dirty pane with the heel of his fist until he had a clear spot through which to look. The fires were clearer now. He could see a few troopers moving about the camp, and the shine of the river in between.

Sitting there in the near darkness, he made a big, bulky shape against the light of the fires in the Army bivouac across the Arkansas. He had graying yellow hair, yellow sideburns, and a stained yellow mustache but no beard. A neatly tied cravat with a stickpin set off his white ruffled shirt, and a gold chain spread across his waistcoat from pocket to pocket with a ponderous elk tooth set in gold dangling from the center of it.

He was a big, raw-boned man who looked out of place in the clothes he wore. He would have looked more comfortable in a laborer's overalls, but he had risen above those workman's clothes and was now Congressman from the new state of Colorado. He represented the district just across the Kansas line.

He had fought and clawed his way up, a slow, patient step at a time, and the ascent had left its marks upon his face. His eyes were hard, cold as bits of winter ice. His mouth was a slash in his weather-reddened face. A tough and able man, he knew all the tricks a politician needs to know, yet he had a certain rugged charm his constituents usually found irresistible.

Tonight, Ben Terborg knew one thing. If the Indians veered west into Colorado it was going to hurt him at the polls, particularly if they burned and pillaged and killed as they went along. Settlers hurt by this north-traveling bunch of renegades were bound to blame their government for allowing it to happen and they would blame their own representatives in particular.

The train came abreast of the camp and jerked to an unsteady halt. The train whistle sounded mournfully, a long blast, then a series of short ones. What that might convey to the troop commander, Terborg didn't know, but it was probably unusual enough to warrant investigation. Particularly in the middle of the night.

Frowning now, he stared into the darkness. He knew which side his political bread was buttered on. Most of the people who had elected him hated Indians. They had suffered at the Indians' hands. So Ben Terborg hated Indians too. But he was also practical, not given to blindly accepting the premise that the government was always right. At the moment he was angry at the government because stupidity had brought this trouble to the land. He was angry because it cost money to chase renegades halfway across the continent — a lot more than it did to feed them properly. And when the Indians left the reservation they endangered Ben Terborg's constituents.

Self-interest, then, was the chief reason Terborg was here. First of all he wanted to see to it that the Indians were caught before they threatened his constituents. Secondly, he figured he could make a campaign issue out of this Indian rebellion and he wanted figures on how much the pursuit of these Cheyenne would cost, including losses sustained by white settlers. He wanted figures on how much feeding the Indians properly would have cost. A comparison might make a fine issue to draw national attention to himself. He might get elected Governor when his term as Congressman ran out. Or Senator. He smiled faintly to himself.

His eyes caught movement across the river. Silhouetted against the fires' light he saw a party of mounted men entering the river and starting the swim across.

Wryly, Ben Terborg reflected that government policy had always seemed to be one of expediency. Each military commander seemed free to formulate his own policy as he went along. It was time the government had a well-defined policy. It was time the Indian wars came to a halt. There was no longer any excuse for them.

Hissing softly, the train sat like a great snake on the rolling, empty plain. The troopers splashed out of the river, climbed the bank and rode toward the small group of men standing beside the locomotive.

The conductor climbed the steps to the first car and walked back to where Terborg was, ignoring the questions other sleepy passengers put to him. He said, "They're here, Congressman."

Terborg got ponderously to his feet. Reaching overhead, he took a heavy, shapeless carpetbag from the rack. He followed the conductor along the aisle and stepped down to the trackside where the troopers were. Speaking to their officer he said, "I'm Congressman Terborg, trooper. Who are you?"

"Lieutenant William Jackson, sir. Do you wish to talk to Captain Rendelbrock?"

"Is he your commanding officer?"

"Yes sir."

Terborg nodded. The lieutenant ordered two of his men to double up, then had the horse thus vacated led to the Congressman. Terborg mounted. His carpetbag in one hand, reins in the other, he followed Lieutenant Jackson toward the riverbank. The conductor called, "Shall we wait for you, Congressman?" and Terborg shouted, "No!"

He heard the hiss of steam, the slow chugging that increased its tempo as the train gained speed. The lieutenant entered the Arkansas, his horse wading out, swimming when his hoofs no longer could touch bottom. Terborg raised his bag to keep it out of the water and followed him. The troopers who had accompanied the lieutenant splashed into the river shallows behind the Congressman.

Once, Lieutenant Jackson looked back, peering through the near darkness as though trying to read the expression on Terborg's face. Terborg called softly, "It's all right, Lieutenant. I'm not afraid."

The horses' feet touched bottom and they lunged out onto the bank. Terborg said, "Wait, Lieutenant. I want to talk to you."

"Congressman, I'd rather . . ."

Terborg's voice turned sharp. "Lieutenant!"

"Yes sir. What is it you wish to know?"

"Send your men ahead."

Jackson issued the necessary order to his men.

One of them, a corporal, saluted, and they trotted their horses away. Terborg dismounted. He sat down on the ground and pulled off a boot. He poured the water out of it and tugged it back on. He repeated the performance with the other boot.

Lieutenant Jackson sat his horse uneasily. Terborg said, "Relax, Lieutenant. Get down and make yourself comfortable."

The lieutenant dismounted. He squatted on his heels and looked at Terborg warily. "Yes sir?"

"What's this damn outbreak all about? What made the Cheyenne break away and head north?"

"They don't like it down south, sir. They like it up on the Yellowstone. That's home to them."

"There has to be more to it than that."

"There is. They've been starved, or half-starved ever since they went down there. A lot of them have died from disease. But mostly, they're plainly homesick, sir, and they claim they were promised they could go back to the Yellowstone if they didn't like it in the south."

"Were they?"

Jackson shrugged. "I don't know, sir. Not officially. No one had the authority I'm sure. But I have no doubt some of the interpreters took it upon themselves to promise a lot of things to get the Cheyenne to agree."

"Then the Indians are probably in the right. Is that what you're trying to say?"

The lieutenant met Terborg's glance steadily. "It is not, sir. I'm a soldier. I do not make statements or decisions. I follow the orders of my superiors."

"But you're in sympathy with the Indians."

"Not officially, sir. Not as a soldier. I think any human being would have to feel sympathy for their predicament. I think any human being would have to admire their courage and their fortitude. But I will fight them, sir, if I encounter them because that's what I am paid to do. I will shoot at them because if I do not, they will shoot at me."

"What kind of man is this Captain Rendelbrock?"

The lieutenant stiffened. "Surely you do not expect me to answer a question like that."

Terborg grinned. "You've already answered it. If you had liked him, you would not have minded saying so."

Lieutenant Jackson got up, walked to his horse and picked up the reins. "I think we had better go on, Congressman. I will take you to the captain."

"Sure, Jackson, sure. I didn't mean to ruffle you. But I came out here to find out the truth and I mean to do it if I can."

"Yes sir." The lieutenant's voice was neutral.

"You don't blame me for that, do you?"

"No sir."

"I won't betray any confidences."

"No sir. Of course not." But Lieutenant Jackson was wavering.

Terborg grinned. "All right, let's go." He put a foot into the stirrup and swung astride. The lieutenant did not mount. He asked unexpectedly, "What, specifically, was it you wanted to know, Congressman?"

Terborg dismounted again. Still holding the horse's reins, he squatted comfortably on the ground. "Start from the beginning. Tell me what happened to make them break out and what has happened since."

Jackson said, "Some of Little Wolf's young men couldn't be held back. They went out on a hunting party and headed north. The agent demanded that Little Wolf call them back. When he said he could not, the agent demanded ten hostages to be ironed and jailed until the young men came back.

"Well, they argued back and forth like they always do. Then the Cheyenne moved their camp against orders, claiming they were going after grass and wood. Troops were sent after them, and surrounded them. They were trying to snare rabbits for food and digging roots. They kept saying they were going north. They had been promised they could and they were going, by God. And go they did, sir, in spite of the troops surrounding them. They slipped away in the night, one at a time, leaving a few behind to tend fires and make it look as though they all still were there."

Terborg interrupted unexpectedly. "Would they have gone if they had been given enough to eat?"

Lieutenant Jackson shook his head. "You've got to understand, Congressman, that these people think for themselves just like we do. They talk things over and they decide democratically. If the majority had wanted to stay, they would have stayed. And if they'd had enough to eat, the majority would have wanted to stay."

"Weren't they treated for these diseases that they caught?"

The lieutenant shook his head. "They had no quinine for their malaria, and nothing for their dysentery. The longer they camped in one place, the worse these two diseases became."

Terborg nodded. "So they got away in the night. How come they weren't caught? Weren't there enough troops to catch them and bring them back?"

Lieutenant Jackson hesitated. When he spoke, it was cautiously. "There were enough troops, sir, but they were slow getting started. It was not known how long the campaign would be, or what kind of resistance might be encountered along the way. Preparations had to be made. The U.S. Army does not travel like a bunch of ragged Indians, sir."

"And there was red tape." Terborg grinned.

"Orders to be issued, sir. Our commanders did not dare move without telegraphing the situation to the Commanding General. Anyway, the pursuit was slow to start and consequently did not catch up with the Indians for several days. Finally we ran into an ambush at Turkey Springs and lost an Arapaho scout and a couple of other men. The Indians slipped away. We caught them the second time at a place called Bear Creek, but they drove us back."

"And you haven't caught up with them since. Is that it?"

"I'm afraid it is, sir."

"What else have the Indians done, besides

whip the U.S. Army twice?"

Lieutenant Jackson's face flushed. He glared briefly at Terborg. "The usual sort of thing. Horses stolen, a few men killed. They drove a bunch of sheep into a lake just for the hell of it. They caught a bunch of buffalo hunters and I don't know why they didn't kill any of them. Just took the buffalo they'd killed and all their guns. The hunters are over there in camp right now. Captain Rendelbrock's holding them. Seems they were hunting south of the Arkansas."

"And the Indians have crossed the Arkansas?"

"Yes sir."

"Any idea how far ahead of you they are right now?"

"Half a day, sir, at least."

"All right, Lieutenant. Thanks." Terborg stood up and mounted. Lieutenant William Jackson followed suit. He looked at Terborg worriedly until Terborg said, "Don't worry, Lieutenant. I'll respect your confidences."

"Thank you, sir."

Terborg followed the lieutenant through the bivouac toward the row of officers' tents beyond, scowling to himself.

# CHAPTER FIVE

Her name was Willow, and she was twenty now. She was tall for an Indian girl, tall even for a Cheyenne. Slender and strong, she walked across the prairie tirelessly, carrying a heavy pack upon her back, leading and some-times carrying a five-year-old child, an orphan since his father had been killed in the Bear Creek fight two days before.

Death was a familiar thing to her. Death was a part of life, an increasingly important part that no Indian could ignore. Death had begun to be a part of Willow's life thirteen years ago in the village of Black Kettle on the bank of Sand Creek. She had been seven then, a plump, happy child, and she had had a family. A father, a mother, two brothers, and a sister younger than she was herself.

Not often did she think of the killing at Sand Creek any more. There were other things to remember, fresher things that had happened since. Yet something about the way the land looked today reminded her of the long trek after the fight, northeastward from the smoldering remains of the village on Sand Creek toward a large and friendly camp of other Cheyenne on the Smoky Hill River.

Since that day she had heard the Sand Creek killing talked about by the old men sitting around their fires. Black Kettle had been told by the soldier chief at Fort Lyon that he could camp on Sand Creek, that he was under the protection of the soldiers there. Yet another band of soldiers had come from another place. They had put guards around Fort Lyon to keep the friendly soldiers from interfering and had then marched upon the unsuspecting village.

In the first gray of dawn, their cannon, emplaced on a bluff behind the village, opened fire without warning of any kind. Grapeshot rattled on the hide tipi coverings like a summer hail. When the people ran out to see what was happening, the muskets of the soldiers opened fire, beating them into the ground the way hail beats down and breaks the grass.

Willow's memory supplied little in the way of details of the fight itself. She recalled the noise, the acrid, biting smell of burning hide tipis and burning flesh. She remembered the wild-eyed, bearded faces of the men who came rushing into the tipi where she was, their guns at ready, their teeth bared ferociously. She had cowered down in her robes, trying not to breathe, trying not to move. Not so her brothers and her sister. They had jumped up and tried to run, only to have their heads smashed like pumpkins by the rifle butts of the whites.

Willow did not know, of course, the words the great bearded soldier chief had spoken to his men just before the dawn attack. "Nits make lice. I want no prisoners!" But she saw the results of those words in her own tipi, and after the soldiers had gone, stared in numbed shock at the smashed and bloody heads of her two brothers and her younger sister. She crept outside, and when the roaring sounds of the battle moved away from the village following the flight of survivors, she ran from those sounds and out onto the snowy prairie all alone.

She traveled aimlessly, suffering from cold, and wet, and the utter terror in her heart. At each sound she cowered down, hiding herself as best she could, scarcely daring to breathe, pretending she was dead. But the sounds were friendly ones, of a bird, or a rabbit, and once of a coyote who ran in fright from the little girl cowering on the ground.

By chance, her path happened to cross the

path of a group of women fleeing the massacre and they took her with them. They bound her partly frozen feet with rags torn from blankets, and fed her some of the hard jerky one of them had found and brought along.

Fearing reprisals from the larger Cheyenne camp on the Smoky Hill, the bearded soldier chief called off the pursuit and took his men back to the place near the mountains from which they had come. The straggling, small groups of survivors were found, and taken in. They were fed, and thawed, and allowed to rest and recover from their wounds.

Willow, whose whole family had been wiped out in a few minutes was adopted by a Dog Soldier named Yellow Wolf, who had two wives and three children of his own.

The years passed, but not many of them, and when Willow was eleven the village in which she lived was attacked again, this time on the Washita by the soldier chief everyone called "Yellow Hair."

Again, the village, which had been promised protection and safety by another soldier chief, was destroyed. George Armstrong Custer took prisoners, though he took no male prisoners over ten years of age.

Willow was among those captured but

was considered too young to be taken to the tents of the soldier chiefs to warm their beds on the cold march back. But many of the girls she knew, some of them no more than three years older than she, were taken by Custer's officers.

Willow was eventually returned to her people along with most of the other captives, and five years later, when she was sixteen, she was taken in marriage by Short Dog, who already had counted three coups against the whites and two against Pawnees.

Her first child was a son, whom they laughingly called Fat Badger because he resembled one. But on the Sappa, three years ago, Short Dog and Fat Badger had been killed. She had not even been able to find their bodies because when she regained consciousness the fires were too hot to be approached.

Why she had not been thrown upon the fires like the others, she would never know. Perhaps by the time they came to her, the soldiers and the dirty, bearded buffalo hunters were too tired from the killing and burning that had gone before. But to this day there was a streak in her hair, the hair grown back white from the bullet scar on her scalp. And there was a knotting of flesh in her upper arm where a bullet had passed on through.

It was not surprising that she hated white men so savagely. She hated the hair that grew on their faces, and their skin, so like the underbelly of a toad. She hated the color of their eyes, like the sky, or like ice in wintertime. And she hated their smell, of tobacco and the sour reek of whisky.

She hated them because they hunted and killed Indians like they did prairie wolves, and she hated them because they took the hides from the buffalo and left the meat, which would have meant life to the starving Cheyenne, to rot upon the plain.

She hated them most, she supposed, for what they had done to the Indians which they had not killed. They had stolen pride from them so that Indian wives crept out of their husbands' tipis at night to lie with the white men for money. They had made of the men complainers who sat in their blankets and fixed their eyes on the past which they knew could never come again. They had stolen from the Cheyenne his courage, without which he was nothing — not as much as the smoke that rises from the fire and dissipates itself in the evening breeze.

Yet now, as she strode across the undulating plain toward the north country so far away, she knew the white men had pushed the Cheyenne too far. They had pushed them until they would be pushed no more. They had taken everything from them that made their lives worthwhile and so had forced them to choose death to life, to rebel and run away toward the north, toward home, regaining at last their pride.

Willow was suddenly proud of this ragged, hungry, sickened people trudging north. She was prouder than she had ever been before. If death came to them, which she believed it would, at least they would have experienced his last bit of glory before they died.

At Turkey Spring, they had beaten the whites and escaped, and at Bear Creek they had beaten them again. But soldiers had been killed and the soldier chiefs angered. There would be more soldiers and more killing up ahead. There would also be killing of whites other than the soldiers. The Cheyenne needed horses and food and guns and powder for the guns and would be forced to kill for them.

The child, the boy, began to lag, though he did not whimper or cry out. Willow smiled and picked him up and carried him effortlessly because he weighed little and was very thin. His eyes seemed enormous in his shrunken face and they drooped now with weariness and he slept. Her own Fat Badger would have been almost as old as this boy was, had he lived, and perhaps this was why she had adopted the boy back there on Bear Creek when his father had been killed.

She looked down at him now, a great tenderness in her eyes, knowing in her heart that he would not live and that she would have him only a little while, but undismayed because the time would be so short. Her own time might be as short, or shorter than that of the little boy. Even now the white men and the soldiers might be planning an ambush up ahead.

But the flooding Arkansas was behind, and the tracks of the great iron horse, and behind also were the fights that had taken place below the Arkansas. Ahead was the Yellowstone and the home of the northern division of the tribe. While Willow had never seen that country she had heard it described pridefully and with reverence by her relatives that belonged to the northern Cheyenne. If they reached that far country alive there would be no more of either the shaking disease or the running disease, and there would be buffalo once more because everyone knew the last remnants of the buffalo lived in the north country on the Yellowstone.

They would camp along some small rushing stream and settle down to live in the good, old way, the men going out to hunt and the women fleshing and tanning robes, or making moccasins and decorating them with dyed quills from the porcupine instead of with the bright glass beads of the white men. Willow herself might please the eye of some warrior who would take her into his lodge. She was still young enough for that.

But such dreaming was for the nights when there was nothing to be done. For now there was the walking, and the carrying of the boy, and the helping of those who were weak and sick and would not make it without her help.

And, sometimes forced upon her against her will, there was the remembering. Always it had been the same, the white soldiers coming out of the dawn, or out of the hazy distance. It had been so three times back there below the Arkansas and it would be so many times in the miles that lay ahead. Each day the columns of the white men grew longer, their white wagons, their horse soldiers, their walking soldiers more numerous. With them there were always the cowboys and the buffalo hunters to add to the hail of bullets falling upon the decimated ranks of the Cheyenne.

Ahead, they would join with the soldier chiefs from the Yellowstone and from the country of the Sioux . . .

In the morning, when the cooking fires were built, their smoke rose straight up into the still air. A few captured horses were driven into camp, some of them wild and bucking, some of them needing a rider clinging to their backs to break them so that they would be usable.

Scouts reported the approach of the soldiers, and now, Little Wolf had a plan. He sent the women and children and the old ones up a long draw that grew shallower as it reached north into the plain, and he followed with the warriors along the canyon of Punished Woman Creek leaving a trail that was broad and plain and tempting to the whites. Where the canyon narrowed down, commanded by a jutting bluff, he placed a few young warriors with instructions to let the soldiers pass unmolested, but to begin shooting when the soldiers tried to retreat.

Little Wolf himself took the main body of Cheyenne warriors on, to stop and wait as though dug in to fight, thereby luring the

52

soldiers past the point where the ambush had been laid.

All this, Willow watched from a high slope of the canyon where she and the others had been sent. She watched, having stationed herself here in case the soldiers bypassed the warriors and threatened the helpless ones hidden just beyond. With her was the boy, shivering a little because of the morning chill and watching her with great, dark eyes.

The soldiers under Lewis came along the canyon, their horses trotting, scouts out ahead but no flankers because Lewis was so sure he could easily whip this small bunch of ragged renegades. The wagons wound around the canyon lip, searching for a place they might descend but not immediately finding it.

And tensely the Cheyenne waited, for the soldiers to pass the ambush point, for the trap to close on them.

The shot came suddenly and unexpectedly, echoing back and forth half a dozen times from the sheer canyon walls. The soldiers, not yet past the ambush point, retreated hastily.

Willow's tense body relaxed with disappointment. It had been a good plan, and would have worked, but now it was spoiled because some young warrior, untried and inexperienced in battle, had fired too soon and ruined everything.

Hastily the soldiers pulled back, then charged up the slope toward that high point where the ambushers were. Little Wolf sent a charge of his own to cover their retreat, the warriors clinging to the sides of their horses where they could not be seen and firing from beneath the horses' necks.

The charge served its purpose and most of the ambushing party got away. Thereafter, the soldiers dismounted from their horses and sent them back to safety with horse-holders, coming on afoot. Above on the plain, a large group of "walks-with-guns" moved around toward the rear of the Cheyenne, their aim to surround and trap them. Yet another group, with scouts leading them, searched for and found the women and the pony herd, hidden in the long, shallow draw behind the Cheyenne men. Sharpshooters began firing down from the canyon run, their bullets kicking up spurts of dust, some hitting horses and either dropping them or sending them galloping away up the canyon in terror, scattering the goods with which they had been packed.

Under the unrelenting pressure of Lewis and his dismounted cavalry, the Cheyenne fell back, fighting for each rock, each foot of ground, but lacking the range that the bullets of the white men had. Back, back, and finally into the long draw where the women and children were.

Here, some of the young men, some of the most reckless ones wanted to charge out and die fighting rather than like rabbits in their holes. Black Crane and Wild Hog stopped them, arrows strong and ready, and the reckless ones fell back sullenly. Afterward, they all waited in the shallow rifle pits, keeping down, admonishing the others also to keep down.

Closer and closer now came the soldiers, encouraged by the soldier chief, Lewis, riding his big Army bay back and forth among them.

Willow stared up at the sun, more than halfway down the western sky. The day had gone swiftly because of the tension and excitement, with the trap set and springing too soon, with the tide of battle, which might have favored the Cheyenne changing because of the spoiled ambush.

She believed she soon would die, and with her the boy, but she was not afraid. Her hand touched the worn handle of the butchering knife at her waist and she made herself a promise that when they killed her it would not be easily.

Closer and closer she saw the dismounted cavalry come, with the soldier chief Lewis standing in his stirrups, yelling at them and waving a pistol in his hand. Closer and closer, while the Cheyenne men huddled down, waiting until the whites should come within effective range of their lightly loaded guns.

Inevitably that time came, while the sun hung like a yellow ball over the western plain. Standing in their rifle pits, the Cheyenne gave back the fire of the whites. Smoke lifted from the battle, rolled toward Willow and hid the fighting shapes of the Cheyenne men.

But she could see the whites, and she saw the big bay horse galloping, his saddle empty now . . .

Back went the white soldiers, their dusty blue coats looking gray in the dying light of the setting sun. Back they went, only to come on again, but this time without the soldier chief Lewis urging them to greater bravery.

Yet under the steady, increasing pressure of their numbers and their inexhaustible supply of powder and bullets and guns, some of the Cheyenne wanted to give up. Willow saw a flash of white down where the men were, and knew someone wanted to surrender and go back.

Surrounded they were, and beaten, yet she could remember that day on the Sappa three years ago when the Cheyenne had tried to surrender to the whites. The whites had shot those who held the white flag, and they had shot women surrendering, their hands held up in the air, and they had shot helpless children when they dropped from their mothers' arms. And some, upon whom they did not wish to waste powder and ball, they had simply clubbed with their rifle butts.

It would be no different now, she told herself fiercely. It would be no different. Could not Little Wolf and the other chiefs see that? If they surrendered now their bodies would burn upon the pyres of their goods just as they had back on the Sappa, three years before.

Fury made her eyes blaze fiercely, made her body weak, made her hands feel cold. "Do not surrender!" she exhorted silently but earnestly with her thoughts, remembering Short Dog and Fat Badger, dead on the Sappa where she herself had been shot and left for dead.

"Do not surrender!" she exhorted and stared at the big-eyed boy who was no more than a shaking rack of bones from the starvation and sickness in the south.

And as though her exhortations and those of others had been heard, the white flags disappeared. The sun slid out of sight in the western plain, staining a few clouds before it died completely, before the gray of dusk crept like a promise of life across the plain and into the shadowed canyon where the Cheyenne were.

The ambulances of the white soldiers rattled over the slope and the canyon floor, gathered up the wounded and the dead, and retreated into the darkness and disappeared. Quiet fell over the canyon where so much blood had been spilled. The Indians built their supper fires in subdued silence and ate in the same quiet way. Husbands looked at their wives and children with gladness showing that once more they had been spared. But in some places there was sorrowful keening for the dead.

All knew there was to be no rest this night. They could not stay, and fight, or they would be overwhelmed. Besides, fighting the whites was not their purpose. Their purpose was to reach the Yellowstone.

When the cooking fires died, they crept silently away, up the long draw that reached far north into the plain, shallowing as it went.

They were headed home, all of them doing what must be done to get them there. They would go peaceably if they could. They would fight if they must. They would steal, or kill if necessary, to get the things they had to have.

# CHAPTER SIX

Since leaving the Sappa, Orvie Watts had traveled almost due south, which was the direction of Dodge City where the bone buyers were. As the contour of the land allowed, he veered slightly east, knowing this land well. He gave no thought to the Indians. They would not come as far east as Dodge.

Memories stirred by the valley of bones and by sight of the Sappa where so many Cheyenne had been killed three years ago stayed alive in his mind a good part of every day. Impatiently he tried to channel his thoughts away from the past but they kept returning in spite of him to the good in his life which was all in the past, to the good which, like the past, was now forever gone.

Orvie had been on his own since running away from home when he was fifteen years old. He didn't often think of the reason he'd run away. He didn't often think of his mother any more.

But he was older now, and he could sometimes think of her nowadays without the hatred that had raged through him at first. Now, a man grown, he could understand —

the aching loneliness she must have felt, loneliness that a fifteen-year-old boy could neither alleviate nor comprehend.

He could think of her without hatred now but never without hurt. Never without a kind of sickness because of what he'd seen.

He worked, those days. He worked and supported the two of them. He worked twelve hours every day in the shoe factory and arrived home well after dark.

But one day he arrived home an hour early because of a boiler explosion at the factory. And he found his mother with a man he had never seen before. He hadn't seen his mother again after that. He'd fled into the winter darkness and had not returned. He'd fled, with her voice crying out to him, crying out her anguish and her pain . . .

That was in Pennsylvania. For the next ten years he wandered along the Eastern seaboard, working both in factories and on farms. His mother never reported him a runaway and he was grudgingly grateful to her for that. So he wasn't bothered by the police.

When he was twenty-five, he came West. That had been twenty years ago, before the war.

Orvie had been then what he was now, a

small, unattractive man who had never been exceptionally good at anything. He wasn't married and he'd never even gone with a girl for very long.

The most adventurous thing he'd ever done was to decide to come West and he had been scared half to death just at the thought of it. But he'd been determined too. He was dissatisfied with his life and with himself.

He made a small stir when he left the little Kentucky town where he lived, riding an old swaybacked horse and leading a mule with everything he owned in the world packed on the old mule's back. Mostly the towns-people scoffed and yelled taunts at him. But it was the first stir he'd ever made and it put a glow into him, a glow that stayed with him for many miles.

He had no clear idea of where he wanted to go. Only West. The word meant many things to him. It meant Indians. It meant a new land in Oregon. It meant the snow-capped peaks of the Rockies and the millions of buffalo that blackened the great, high plains. It meant adventure, danger, perhaps even death.

It also meant endless, monotonous days of traveling. It meant being alone until you got to talking to your goddam horse and mule so you wouldn't talk to yourself. It meant sitting at a rough-hewn bar in some frontier saloon and drinking until you fell off the stool onto the sawdust door — just because you were so damn glad to have someone to talk to that you didn't care. It meant women, available even to Orvie if he had the price.

Eventually it meant something else — acceptance such as Orvie Watts had never known before — and would never know again.

It had been late spring in 1858. May, Orvie thought. Driving a freight wagon, one of a train of wagons, he arrived at Bent's Fort on the Arkansas.

It was strange the way things happened to a man. Strange the way unexpected little things could change a man's whole life. Something had spooked the mules as he was climbing down. They hadn't moved far, but they'd thrown him off balance and made him fall. His leg bone snapped as he struck the ground.

A stupid accident. He had often wondered what his life might have been like if he had not fallen and broken his leg that day.

But he had and it had forced him to stay at Bent's Fort instead of returning with the wagon train. After a couple of days he'd been able to get up and hobble around on a home-made crutch, and after that he'd spent a lot of time sitting on the gallery in the sun, waiting for the bone to knit.

Indians, numerous both in and around Bent's Fort, suddenly and unexpectedly became people to him instead of half-naked savages.

The Cheyenne were a friendly people. They had been friendly with the Bents for many years, trusting them, trading with them. Some of the Bents had married into the tribe, choosing the free, good life of the Indian in preference to the life of the whites.

There were horse races every day just outside the fort. Betting was always hot and heavy between Indians and whites, between Indians and Indians and between whites and whites. Every time there was a race, Orvie hobbled out to watch, and bet. Gradually he began to spend as much time in the Indian villages as he did at the fort. Then ending was, of course, inevitable. He met an Indian girl . . .

Her name was Young Deer, and she was sixteen at the time. Orvie courted her briefly, then presented her father with horses and firearms. A lodge was prepared for them and when they occupied it, they were man and wife according to Cheyenne law.

By mid-July, the bone in Orvie's leg had knit, although the leg was stiff and not quite as straight as it had been before. The village moved, north and east to the Smoky Hill River where they camped again.

There followed days of unbelievable happiness for Orvie Watts, days of riding out to hunt deer in the brush-grown river bottoms where the beaver dams made wide and placid pools. There were days of sitting on the edge of some such pool fishing, or just dozing and sometimes staring at the puffy white clouds drifting in the sky.

And the nights. The nights he would remember always with pain that was like a sharp knife in his heart. Young Deer had been all any man could ever want, and she had loved him desperately. He knew that now, knew it now that it was many years too late.

Brown and beautiful and warm, she slept close to him each night. Each morning when he awoke it would be to her smile as she moved around the lodge preparing his breakfast for him.

Evenings he would watch her deft, small hands as they did quillwork on a shirt or pair of moccasins and occasionally would catch her glance, warmly raised to his.

For the first time since running away from home, Orvie Watts knew what it was to love and be loved. He was accepted without question by the band. If he wished to participate in a raid or hunt, he was free to do so. If he did not, no one minded or indeed even noticed it.

By a white man's standards, it was an indolent life. There was much time for doing nothing, time for a man to think.

Too much time, perhaps. Too much time for distrusting a life that seemed a bit too good to be altogether true.

Now, sitting high on the jolting seat of the bone wagon, he shook himself visibly and cursed sourly beneath his breath. Damn it, all that was gone and past. Why did it have to keep coming back and tormenting him? Young Deer was dead and he had killed her himself and that was that.

Ahead there was a stream, winding through a tree-grown cut in the flat prairie. His practiced eye selected the easiest place to cross and he headed directly for it.

Down through the trees he went, and suddenly found himself face to face with four Indian braves. He hauled the wagon to a halt. The mules snorted, rolled their eyes and laid back their ears.

For what seemed a long, long time Orvie and the Indians eyed each other silently. Orvie knew one of them and saw an answering gleam of recognition in the Indian's eyes.

The man was about Orvie's age and was called Lame Bear. In the Cheyenne tongue, Lame Bear said, "We want the mules. And we want your guns."

Orvie felt anger rise in him. Loss of the mules would mean loss of the wagons and the bones, because chances were they wouldn't be here by the time he walked to civilization, got more mules and came back for them. Loss of the bones meant the loss of two months' work. He said, "Lame Bear speaks like a fool. If you take the mules the soldiers will come after you."

Lame Bear laughed contemptuously. "The soldiers are already after us." He stared at Orvie coldly, and Orvie could see that he was remembering . . .

He stooped and grabbed for the rifle lying on the floorboard at his feet. Straightening, he saw the tomahawk as it left Lame Bear's hand. It struck him full in the forehead. The day turned black instantly and his mouth tasted sourly of brass. He felt himself falling but he did not feel the impact when he limply struck the ground . . .

The wagon John was driving, traveling nearly a hundred yards behind, now came through the trees. John saw Orvie lying on the ground and saw the four Cheyenne braves. He grabbed for his own rifle, also on the floorboards beneath his feet.

The range this time was too great for a tomahawk throw. Lame Bear raised his gun . . .

John's rifle came up. He opened his mouth as though to shout, but no sound came out.

Lame Bear fired. Behind him, the other three were scattering, driving their short-legged ponies to right and left to avoid John's bullet.

But John's gun fired almost straight up into the air as Lame Bear's bullet caught him squarely in the chest. He was driven back off the wagon seat to sprawl loosely on the load of bones.

The mules started to bolt, but two of the Indians rode in, each catching a headstall and stopping them. Lame Bear pushed his reluctant horse close to the wagon, caught John's boot and dragged him off the load of bones. John's body hit the ground inertly, like a sack of grain, rolled a little and laid quite still.

Already the Indians, with the exception of

Lame Bear, were slashing harness to free the mules. As they were freed, the mules trotted away, stopping, grouping, and staring back in puzzlement at the Indians.

Lame Bear got John's rifle from the wagon bed, then rode to the wagon Orvie had been driving. Orvie's rifle lay on the ground. Lame Bear dismounted and picked it up. After that he slid the revolver from Orvie's holster and looked at it. Kneeling, he unbuckled the cartridge belt from around Orvie's waist. He could hardly have failed to notice that Orvie's chest still rose and fell, but he paid no heed.

Rising, Lame Bear swung to his horse's back. He thundered away, with the other three following. The mules ran as he approached and he and the others turned them expertly and headed them toward the southwest. They raised a thin plume of dust that settled slowly in the still autumn air.

Cut harness and bone wagons sat forlornly in the little grove of trees, invisible from the surrounding plain. The Cheyenne had been kinder to John than had the Kiowas. The tongueless mute was dead, his chest a mass of dark-clotted blood. But Orvie Watts still lived. He lay flat on his back, his face turned upward toward the sky, his breath coming slow but regular.

There was a blue knot on his forehead, from which a small trickle of blood had spilled and dried. He was covered with dust and his hat had come off his head. But he was still alive.

At sundown, Orvie stirred, groaned a little and opened his eyes. They had a flat, uncomprehending look, a look of complete unawareness and puzzlement. He moved his head and immediately winced with the violent pain the movement caused.

The merciless pounding went on, blurring his mind, twisting his memory so that the past suddenly loomed up to confront him. It had been almost twenty years.

Had it really been that long? They had passed very swiftly, those intervening years for all that they had been filled with sweat and dust and blood and the stink of death.

There was pain in remembering, but he couldn't fight it any more. He couldn't keep the past from crowding back into his thoughts.

All of that first autumn, Orvie had been content to stay close to home. A couple of raiding parties went out to steal horses from the Pawnees, but he did not accompany them. He hunted only enough to keep meat in his lodge. He fished sometimes for his own pleasure and because he himself liked fish. He occasionally raced the fastest of the half-dozen horses that he owned. And the other Cheyenne smiled at the way he stayed close to Young Deer and to his own lodge, knowing this was always the way of a newly married man.

Snow whirled out of the north, driven on a blizzard wind. It filled the dry gullies of the plain, and lay deep in the villages of the Cheyenne. Cold froze the water in the streams until the people had to chop holes in it so that they could bathe each morning. The women had to break the crust of ice before they could get water for their cooking.

But the village was snug beneath a high, gray bluff lying to the north of it and therefore breaking the worst force of the wind. And the tipis themselves were warm, the fires glowing red in their centers, the smoke rising lazily to the smoke holes at their peaks. And when the cold was worst, there were the warm, soft buffalo robes, through which the most bitter cold could not penetrate.

Young Deer began to swell with child, and a new, softly contented look came into her face. The months fled past so swiftly that it was spring before Orvie realized it.

Now, his own mind accepted the Indian way at last, completely, as he had never accepted it before. He realized that when he first had come to live with the Cheyenne, it had been with reservations and with doubts. He had known he could leave if it did not work out.

But he had put aside his reservations and his doubts. His hair, which had grown long during the winter months, he braided in the Cheyenne way, though the braids were short. His skin, from daily exposure to the sun, was as brown as that of any Cheyenne brave. He wore the deerskin clothing of the Cheyenne, clothing which Young Deer had made for him. He rode bareback the way the Cheyenne did and was growing proficient in the use of bow and arrow, and also in the throwing of the tomahawk.

In June, Young Deer gave birth — to a lusty boy whose voice filled the lodge and echoed along the village street. And Orvie Watts smiled with a strong, sure pride.

He went out with the others for the summer hunt, while the child was not yet two weeks old. And Young Deer stayed at the village, though many of the women came along on the hunt, to do the work of butchering and the drying of the hides.

These were the first buffalo Orvie Watts

had killed, great, shaggy beasts that he killed by racing his horses alongside of them as they ran and shooting his arrows or plunging his lance into their necks. It was sometimes dangerous, but it was exhilarating and made his blood run fast and hot.

The hunt was a great success, for the white men had not yet killed enough of the buffalo to make much difference. Laden with meat and hides which they transported on travois poles, the hunters returned to the village triumphantly.

But there were rumors in the village when Orvie Watts returned. Ugly rumors told behind the hand covering the mouth, told with little, knowing smiles. Rumors of a brave named Beaver who sat before Orvie's lodge while he was gone, who walked with Young Deer when she went to the stream for water, who, perhaps, did other things as well.

Orvie heard the rumors and instantly there was a picture in his mind. It was a picture of another betrayal, of his mother with a man he had never seen before. He accused Young Deer furiously.

She denied wrongdoing tearfully, and the baby screamed with terror when Orvie came near to him, and Orvie stamped out into the summer night, believing the rumors now, driven to believe by the memory of that other betrayal so long ago. They were all alike, he told himself bitterly. They were all alike. God damn their souls to hell, women were all alike!

Orvie left the village, riding as though possessed by evil spirits, gouging the frightened horse with his heels and beating him over the rump with his rifle barrel. Off from the village he went, and up into the broken hills lying north of it. He rode the horse this way until he faltered and fell and then shot the animal in a fit of rage because he was left out here afoot.

After that, he walked, and ran, and when he was hungry he stalked and killed a deer. All the while that old horror grew more graphic in his mind. Only now his mind saw Young Deer with a stranger on their bed of robes.

Imagination worked at his mind like a crawling worm. All his friends, all the villagers, were in reality laughing at him behind his back. They had known about Young Deer's infidelity all along, he thought. Yet they had not told him but had waited for him to find out by himself.

And so the mind of Orvie Watts, nourished by suspicion, twisted by the shock out of his childhood, seeking to vindicate his own manhood, decided Young Deer was guilty and sentenced her to die. And once having decided that, proceeded to carry out the sentence it had passed.

Returning, he became as crafty as the hunting weasel, knowing the Cheyenne would suspect him of this if they knew he had returned. Like a thief he crept back to the village at night, slipping into it silently and without arousing any of the guards.

He had doubts as he returned, a sharp knife in his hand. What if Young Deer was not guilty at all? What if she were true to him, and had been true all along?

Ruthlessly he put these doubts away from him. No longer, he told himself, would any man, or indeed any women either, laugh at him. He would show them what happened to those who betrayed Orvie Watts.

Silently he crept along the village street. Dogs came out and barked at him, but fell silent when they caught his scent and recognized him as belonging here. Straight to the entrance flap of his own lodge he went, and entered, and paused to look around and let his eyes become accustomed to the darkness.

Over on the far side of the tipi, Young Deer moved and sighed in her sleep, and he crossed to her, wondering if he would catch

Beaver lying with her right here in his own lodge tonight.

But she was alone, except for the baby, who was also sleeping peacefully. And Orvie stood there looking down, hearing the faint, sweet sounds of their breath, and pausing for a moment, wondering.

Suddenly it was not Young Deer lying here at all. He was a boy again and this was his mother . . . Shuddering violently, he knelt and plunged the sharp knife home . . .

Afterward he got up and ran, straight to the tipi of Beaver, where he used the knife again and again. Then leaving everything behind but his rifle, the knife and the clothes he wore, he crept out onto the prairie. A Cheyenne who kills another Cheyenne is outcast forever and doomed to wander the prairie alone.

But Orvie Watts didn't need the Cheyenne. He was white, and could return to the whites. There were no penalties among the whites for killing a couple of Cheyenne Indians. The white man's law wouldn't even care.

Orvie traveled north and west to the new settlement on the bank of Cherry Creek. He cut his hair and bought white man's clothing and got himself a job driving a freight wagon between Denver City and

Julesburg Station, northeast of Denver on the plains.

He didn't think of the son he had left behind in the village of the Cheyenne. He told himself that son was the fruit of Young Deer's infidelity, and not his at all. Yet even while he told himself this, he knew he lied. The boy was his.

These things, then, were the memories that twisted Orvie Watts's expression sometimes when the past came flooding back, when some smell, or breath of spring wind, or warmth of sun upon his naked chest reminded him. He opened his eyes now, and rolled, and stared at the moon looking so coldly down at him. His head ached, both from the blow of the tomahawk and from his memories. He wondered why Lame Bear had not killed him. He'd recognized him sure enough.

He struggled to his feet. If Lame Bear was with the fleeing Cheyenne, others who had been in the village long ago might be with them too. His son the baby he had left when he killed Young Deer might even be along. The boy would be . . . Good God, he would be nineteen now, a man!

Suddenly he knew something else, that he would never consciously admit to himself before. He had been wrong. Young Deer had not been unfaithful to him. She had been true, and he was a murderer, a spoiler who had killed the one person in all the world who had loved him and whom he had loved.

Doggedly Orvie tramped south while the night slipped past. Dawn grayed the horizon in the east, and the rising sun stained the clouds violet, then pink, then gold, before it poked its shining rim above the plain. Small flocks of birds rose out of the grass in front of Orvie, circled him and alighted again after he had passed.

He began to bear slightly right, heading for a line of gray sandstone bluffs half a dozen miles away. Squinting his eyes both against the glare of the sun and the pain in his head, sorefooted from walking, he limped along steadily.

# CHAPTER SEVEN

From the bivouac on the bank of Sappa Creek, Lieutenant Robert Mannion led his small troop south at dawn of the day following. Straight and tall he rode, a handsome man with blue eyes, reddish hair and a flowing, red, cavalry-style mustache.

There was gentleness about Mannion's eyes and mouth that made him a favorite with the ladies wherever he happened to be, on whatever Army post, yet this gentleness was not to be mistaken for softness. He was a good soldier. He had been with General Crook on the Rosebud in '76, two years before, and had been decorated for his actions there. He'd been told to warn the settlers in this area and then scout south, warning settlers as he did, until he made contact either with Colonel Lewis, his own commanding officer, or with Captain Rendelbrock out of Fort Reno in Indian Territory.

On the fourth day, near dusk, Corporal Delaney came galloping toward the lieutenant, leaning low over the withers of his horse. He pulled the plunging animal to a halt, saluted briefly and reported, "Them bone wagons . . . I told you about 'em, sir . . . they're abandoned over there in that draw. Harness is cut an' there's a grave . . ."

Mannion nodded. "Let's go." He raised an arm, motioning the men behind him to follow, and galloped after Delaney, who hauled his horse to a halt short of the bone wagons and upwind from them.

A shift of wind carried Mannion the smell, the gagging, sweetish smell of decaying flesh. He held his face in a rigid mold, refusing to show his men that he had noticed it. He dismounted, walked to the grave and stared down at it. He glanced at Delaney. "How many did you say there were?"

"Two, sir. One was a mute — had his tongue cut out by Kiowas, the other said. The other one was middle-aged — kind of short."

"Scout around for trail and see what you can find."

"The mules, sir?"

Mannion shook his head. "We know where they went. Look for a man's trail — a man afoot."

Delaney rode away, beginning a circle of the camp. The other men shifted around until their horses were upwind from the bone wagons. One of them said, "How the hell does a man stand that, day after day? How the hell does he eat? Just a whiff of it makes me want to puke."

A small smile touched Lieutenant Mannion's mouth. He'd been wondering the same thing himself. He supposed a man got used to it. Maybe he got so used to it he couldn't even smell it any more.

It was plain enough to him what had happened here. Three Indians had intercepted the bone wagon. They'd killed one of the drivers, then had slashed the harness and released the mules. Indians didn't like mules as well as horses but the Cheyenne were in no position now to be choosy. They'd driven off the mules. They might have taken the other driver with them, but Mannion doubted it. The second man had probably been wounded and left to die. Only he'd managed to travel . . .

Delaney shouted, "Here it is, Lieutenant!"

Mannion turned his head. Delaney sat his horse at the foot of the cutbank. He rode to the corporal, who pointed at tracks climbing the bank, at sloughed-off earth at its top. Mannion said, "All right, we'll camp here tonight. We can't find him in the dark."

"I could ride out half a mile or so, Lieutenant. Could be he didn't travel far."

Mannion nodded. "All right, do that. But be careful you don't run into Indians."

"Yes sir." Delaney put his horse up out of the ravine and galloped away in the direction the trail had gone.

Mannion returned to the other men. He grinned. "Move upwind far enough so that this smell won't bother us."

# CHAPTER EIGHT

When he first heard about the Cheyenne
from Corporal Delaney, Morgan had felt no
particular alarm. He had known it was possible, even probable, that they wouldn't get
this far. Even if they did, there were dozens of
other routes they could take to get to the Yellowstone.

But when he talked to Lieutenant
Mannion — when he found out they were
less than a week away . . . That was different. If they'd got across the Arkansas
without being stopped, no telling how far
they might come. He knew this was the
most likely route for them to take.

Everything Morgan Cross possessed was
rooted in the land on Calf Creek where his
house and ranch buildings were. He'd be a
fool if he relied on the Army to protect his
place for him. He turned his horse west
toward Cut-Nose Creek, where Ned
Murphy and his two sons lived.

Cut-Nose Creek was a dry stream bed
that wound south to terminate in the valley
of the Sappa, as Calf Creek did. The only
difference was that Calf Creek had water in

it, most years enough to irrigate the hay. Cut-Nose Creek was dry except in spring when the weather was wet anyway, and occasionally in summer when there would be a cloudburst somewhere along its course.

The distance from the site of the Sappa killing, sometimes called Cheyenne Hole, to the Murphy place was nearly twenty-five miles. Cross rode it at a steady trot all the way but he did not arrive until well after dark. The Murphys had obviously also been warned about the Indians because the lamps went out while he was still a hundred yards from the house — as soon as the old collie barked.

He yelled, "It's Morgan Cross!" The dog stopped barking and followed Morgan's horse, wagging his tail lazily. At the door, Cross swung down. A match flared in the kitchen, illuminating Ned Murphy's skinny, stooped shape in the doorway and the shape of his oldest son immediately behind.

Murphy said, "You're in time for supper, Morg. Come in and sit." He turned away, lighted a lamp and lowered the chimney over the burning wick.

Morgan went in. The kitchen was warm, steamy from the cooking and fragrant with the smell of it. He felt a twinge of guilt, wondering if Nellie was waiting supper for him.

Ned Murphy put the lamp down in the center of the table and began to carry food from the stove. Morgan took a place between Murphy two sons, Will and Ben. Ben, the younger and just a little older than Morgan's Jess, asked excitedly, "That trooper stop at your place, Mr. Cross?"

Cross nodded.

"Did he tell you about them Cheyenne comin' up from Indian Territory down south of here?"

"He told me." Murphy handed him a pot of stew and he ladled some onto his plate. The boy persisted, "You reckon they'll get this far?" There was excitement in Ben's shining eyes. "Boy! I'd like to get me one of 'em!" He caught Morgan's steady glance on him and added guiltily. "Was they to jump us here, I mean. I wouldn't just shoot 'em to be shootin'."

Morgan felt like taking issue with the boy and was surprised at himself. Maybe he was just plain contrary today, ready to argue with anybody about anything. Early this morning he'd damn near had words with that bone picker over two stinking wagonloads of bones.

Murphy asked bluntly and without much warmth, "What are you doing over here, Morg? You want something from me?"

Cross yanked his thoughts back to the present and to this place. He stared at Murphy, who was frowning at him resentfully. He felt like lashing out at Murphy, but instead he said, "I came over to see if you and your boys would come to my place and stay until this Indian scare is over with."

"What about our place? You trying to say your house is more valuable than ours?"

Morgan deliberately took a big mouthful of stew and chewed it before answering. He swallowed and took a gulp of coffee before he said, "That ain't what I figured at all. You ought to know me better'n that. What I figured was that the Cheyenne would probably come by Cheyenne Hole on their way. They'll stop long enough to get themselves all stirred up and then they'll head north again. The first ranch they'll hit after leaving Cheyenne Hole is my place, and you know what they'll do to it."

"What if they don't come that way? How do you know . . . ?"

"I don't," Morgan Cross said patiently. "But if they don't come that way, they ain't likely to be in a burning mood, are they?"

Still Murphy hesitated. Morgan said, "I don't expect nobody to put in their time for nothing. A dollar a day for you and half a dollar a day for each of your boys."

The faces of the two boys brightened immediately. Ben asked excitedly, "Can we do it, Pa? Can we?"

Murphy nodded. He glanced at Morgan Cross and said grudgingly, "Forget what I said a minute ago, Morg. I guess you ain't like that."

Morgan nodded easily. "I've already forgot it, Ned."

"When do you want us over there?"

"I'll come by here on my way back home. It'll likely be a couple of days from now. The trooper said the Cheyenne were still a week away," Morgan replied.

"All right. We'll be ready."

Morgan led his horse across the yard to the corral, unsaddled him and turned him in. Murphy threw him down a couple of forks of grass hay from the loft.

In silence, the pair walked back to the house. The boys were just finishing up with the dishes. Murphy said, "Take that same bed you always do."

Cross thanked him, went into the tiny bedroom and sat down on the bunk to remove his boots. He stripped to his underwear, got under the blankets and closed his eyes. In ten minutes he was asleep. In the morning he was gone before Ned Murphy and his sons awoke.

# CHAPTER NINE

The days passed slowly and uneventfully for Nellie Cross. Morgan did not return, but it was not the first time he had failed to return for several days and she supposed he had gone to Julesburg again.

On the fourth evening, a strange unease unaccountably possessed Nellie Cross. She went outside and stared at the empty land. Had something happened to Morgan? she wondered. Or did she have some sixth sense warning about Indians? Could they have come this far so soon?

She retreated into the house and locked the door. She hurried the children off to bed, then sat in the darkened kitchen staring uneasily out of the window. Something was out there, she realized. Something out there had suddenly made her afraid.

It could be a white renegade, of course, an outlaw passing through. If that was what it was, he'd probably steal a horse and go on without bothering anyone in the house. But it could also be Indians. They would want horses too. But they'd want food as well.

She wasn't really afraid of them, she

firmly told herself. No matter how many there were. Indians knew better nowadays than to hurt a white person, particularly a woman or her children. Retribution for doing so would be swift and certain and terrible.

Time dragged slowly past. When she heard the horses begin to nicker and gallop around the corral, she got Morgan's shotgun from the far corner of the kitchen and loaded it. She sat down facing the door, waiting, now trembling.

They would take the horses, she told herself. They would take the horses and go away. It had to be Indians, she realized. Only Indians and their strange, wild smell, would frighten the horses that way.

Suddenly there was a thunderous knocking on the kitchen door. She called, "Go away! I have a gun. I'll use it if I must."

The knocking stopped. She heard voices, men's voices; but they were muffled and she could not tell whether they belonged to Indians or to whites. Again it was silent, ominously so.

They were still there. She'd heard no racket of departure, no yelling, no thunder of horses' hoofs. But what were they doing now?

Trembling, she sat very still, the shotgun

across her knee. She heard a creaking on the stairs, turned her head and saw the shadowy forms of her three children creep into the room, the two girls wearing their white nightgowns, Jess wearing a pair of dark pants he had hastily put on over his white nightshirt. He whispered, "What's the matter, Ma?" his voice hoarse with fear of the unknown.

"Someone's out there, Jess. They're after the horses, I think."

"Indians?"

"I don't know. Probably."

The younger of the two girls, Hope, began to cry. Nellie reached out and pulled the child close to her. Hope buried her face in her mother's breast, whimpering.

Suddenly Nellie had an almost uncontrollable desire to laugh. At the irony of this. At the cruelty of life itself. For seven years she had refused Morgan because she was afraid of death. Afraid of childbirth. She had all but driven him away from her.

Now death was closer than it had ever been to her. There were Indians out here, angry Indians, hungry Indians, Indians who had been starved and cheated and robbed and who would strike back at whites wherever they were found.

They wanted horses but they wanted so

much more. They wanted guns to replace those which had been taken from them by the soldiers when they were shipped south more than a year ago. They wanted clothing for themselves and for their women and children. They wanted food. They were aware that white men kept their guns inside the house. Their guns and clothing and their food. Only potatoes and root vegetables were kept outside the house.

Nellie pushed Hope away from her. She knew what she had to do. She stood up, saying firmly to the children, "Go upstairs to bed. I am going to let them in and give them food." She put her hands on Jess's shoulders. "Don't come down no matter what happens and don't let the girls come down. Is that clear, Jess? Will you do what I tell you to?"

She sensed the doubt in him. His thin shoulders were trembling and he drew in a long, shuddering breath. "Yes, Ma," he said reluctantly.

Nellie herded the children away from her, toward the hall and the stairs beyond. "Go on then. Hurry."

The two little girls ran. Jess followed more slowly, almost hesitantly as if wondering if he was doing what he should. She waited until the sounds died away, then fumbled her way to the table and struck a match. She raised the lamp chimney, touched the match to the wick, lowered the chimney again.

No shots ripped through the window, none through the door. She unloaded the shotgun and replaced it where it had been before. She was defenseless now but she knew it had to be that way. They were much more likely to shoot if she had a gun in her hands than if she did not.

Trembling violently, cold from her feet to her throat, she crossed the kitchen to the door. She raised the bar, stood for a moment hesitating, then flung the door wide. She stood there, illuminated by the lighted lamp on the table behind her, and said, "Come in. You may have our guns and food. You may have anything you want."

She smelled them immediately, a greasy, wild smell that came from their leather clothing and greasy hair. She saw them crowding toward her, and stepped aside.

They were wild, she thought, like the animals who lived out on the wide, flat plain. There were four of them, all younger than Morgan was. One of the four did not look to be more than sixteen or seventeen years old. They crowded into the kitchen, sniffing, grunting, making animal-like sounds as they communicated with each other in the Cheyenne tongue.

The oldest of the four, who might have been close to thirty, she supposed, crossed to where the shotgun leaned against the wall and picked it up. He looked at it, saw that it was unloaded and glanced at her questioningly. She pointed soundlessly to the table, where she had put the loads, the paper cartridges, the percussion caps. Immediately he crossed to the table, snatched them up and loaded the gun. He said, "More guns."

She lighted another lamp with hands that trembled almost uncontrollably. Carrying it, she went into the parlor. She put the lamp down on the table and opened the closet door. Instantly the Indian who had followed her shoved her aside. He threw out almost everything that was in the closet before he found what he was looking for — a single-shot, large bore percussion rifle and a Colt's percussion revolver Morgan had discarded when he bought his newer, cartridge revolver a year ago in Julesburg. The Indian gave her a shove toward the kitchen and she went back there, the Indian following along behind.

The other Indians had made a shambles of the place. One had a piece of canvas laid out on the floor and was filling it with various items of food — a sack of coffee beans, loose navy beans, dried peas and apples, raisins. Another had found a flour sack and a sack of salt. The third said harshly, "Blankets."

It was something she had not thought about. The blankets were all upstairs where the children were. She said, "My children are up there. I'll go get the blankets for you, but you can't come upstairs."

They stared at her impassively, and she doubted if they had understood. Speaking slowly and emphasizing each word, she said, "I get blankets for you. I get. You stay." She felt foolish speaking that way to them but she had to make them understand. It would frighten the children to death if they came upstairs with her.

Not one of the four answered. Two kept busy loading up on food. A third was examining the guns he had gotten from the parlor closet a few minutes before. The fourth just stared at her.

She said patiently and slowly, "If I was going to shoot you, I would have done it a while ago, wouldn't I? I wouldn't give you all the guns in the house and then go upstairs for another one to shoot you with."

She didn't know if they were tormenting her or if they really did not understand. The older one repeated, "Get blankets. I go, too."

She shook her head stubbornly. "You will not! And the four of you can just get out of here. If you won't let me go up alone and get the blankets, then by Heaven you can do without! Now get!" She snatched up the broom and advanced threateningly with it.

The older Indian grinned at her. She swung the broom but he evaded it easily, grinning still. He moved toward the hall and the stairway like a cat.

She tried to follow, but another of the Indians caught and held her with hands that bit cruelly into her arms. The smell of him was overpowering now, his breath hot in her face.

He was only holding her, but suddenly all the stories she had heard about women mistreated by the Plains Indians came back to her. She would be staked out on the ground while one after the other of them used her like an animal. Her children would be forced to watch while she was raped . . .

She screamed suddenly, a lost, awful sound that reverberated through the house and out through the open door onto the plain beyond. With her scream, the last dam of restraint broke within her mind. Scream after scream tore from her mouth until the

Indian brave clamped a callused, greasy hand down over it to shut her up.

She bit the hand, and was cuffed ferociously for doing so. She began to struggle, trying to break free, but was held inexorably against his body by one encircling arm while the other clamped itself again over her now bloody mouth.

There were only the faint sounds of struggle here in the kitchen and the creak of the Indian's feet on the stairs. But suddenly there was also a boy's scared, immature voice, "You get back down there and out of our house or I'll shoot!"

She bit the Indian's hand savagely and when it was withdrawn screamed, "Jess! No!" remembering the twenty-two rifle his father had bought him for his birthday. The twenty-two cracked and there was a startled grunt from the Indian on the stairs. The shotgun roared, its awful sound filling every corner of every room in the house. After that there was no further sound from upstairs, only the continuing creak of the stair steps as the Indian climbed toward the top.

Nellie Cross was hysterical now. She knew Jess was dead, that the girls were probably dead too, or soon would die. She herself would die. There was no hope now, no longer any hope.

She felt her senses slipping away from her and did not resist. She slumped in the Indian's arms and the man let her slide limply to the floor, plainly glad to be rid of her. The Indian who had gone upstairs now returned, carrying hastily snatched blankets in his arms. One of the other Cheyenne now seized the edge of the stove and heaved, spilling its red-hot coals upon the wooden floor. A tongue of flame licked up . . .

The Cheyenne seized the things they had come for, the canvas filled with food, the guns, the blankets. They ran out of the house into the night and climbed onto their ponies awkwardly because of the burdens they were carrying.

The kitchen was lighted by the flames in it now. Smoke had filled the entire house and was pouring up the staircase in a column as if the stairway was a gigantic flue, over the bloody body of Jess, into the room where the two little girls still lived.

They began to cough, and choke. Tears streamed from their eyes. Hope screamed, "Mama! Mama!"

Their room, directly over the kitchen, began to grow hot. The floorboards began to smoke from the awful heat below.

Gradually the two little girls stopped coughing and lay on the bed as though in a stupor. Their eyes closed. Their breathing stopped.

Outside, one of the Cheyenne killed the calf and loaded it on his horse. They opened the corral and drove the horses out. The animals thundered away, with the Cheyenne in pursuit.

Behind, the Cross house was a gigantic torch. Flames leaped forty feet into the black night sky. Sharp sounds like pistol shots filled the air from the burning wood.

The milch cow bawled continuously in terror as smoke from the house began to drift into the barn.

# CHAPTER TEN

It was three days instead of two before Morgan Cross returned to the Murphy place on Cut-Nose Creek, but with him rode half a dozen men, the Calloways from up in Nebraska on the Republican, the Rittenhouses from the North Fork of the Solomon, and Dave Gray, a wolfer who worked sometimes for the Rittenhouses and others but who lived in a tiny sod shack between the North Fork of the Solomon and the Republican.

They rode in a little after noon, and hunkered down on their heels with their backs to the corral fence, smoking and talking, until Ned Murphy called them for a hastily prepared noon meal.

They had finished the meal, and their cigars, before they saw the smoke.

Twenty miles, it was, from the Murphy place on Cut-Nose Creek, to the Cross Place on Calf Creek. Twenty miles as a crow flies. It was Chet Rittenhouse who stood up, raised a hand to shade his eyes from the overhead sun and asked, "Hey! What could be burnin' over there?"

All heads turned to follow his pointing

arm because fire could be a terrible thing on the plains and was almost always to be feared. Morgan Cross stood up, his face losing its color, his eyes pinching down as though a pain had suddenly struck through his head.

Chet turned his head and looked at Cross. His voice was now subdued. "That's about where your place is, ain't it, Morg?"

Morgan Cross was moving, running toward his horse tied to one of the corral poles. He didn't remember untying the reins, didn't remember vaulting to the horse's back, but the horse was running, running toward that tiny, almost insignificant plume of smoke that, under other circumstances, might have gone unnoticed and unmarked.

Behind him he heard the yelling voices of the other men and, after several moments, the thunder of their horses' hoofs as they followed him. He leaned low over the withers of his horse, praying with lips that moved but with no sound coming out.

His mind saw Nellie, as she had been on their wedding day, all in white, with a white veil covering her face. He saw the pink flush of confusion on her face when he lifted the veil, and the promise of her eyes. He saw her heavy with child, her face calm and placid the way a woman's face gets when she is carrying.

He saw Jess, his son, sturdily carrying the milk bucket from the barn, or driving the cow in to be milked, or trying to hold the plow steady as old Duke pulled it through Nellie's vegetable patch behind the house.

And the little girls. He smelled their clean, starched fragrance and felt the softness of their hair as they snuggled close to him, one on each strong knee. He saw the petal-softness of their baby mouths, and the blue vagueness of their baby eyes, so like the eyes of a new-born fawn.

He knew what he would find where the plume of smoke rose into the noonday sky. He knew what he would find. That was not a thick column of smoke from a fiercely burning, freshly kindled blaze. It was a thin sifting up of smoke, coming from coals and ashes long since burned. Except for the almost unbelievable clarity of this early autumn day, Chet Rittenhouse would not have seen the smoke at all.

Twenty miles. In the first mile he outdistanced the men coming along behind. He faintly heard their shouts but he paid no heed to them. He spurred his horse mercilessly, until blood ran from the horse's flanks and stained his spurs. He kept on spurring until foam covered the horse's neck and shoulders, until his lungs heaved like a gigantic bellows, and very audibly.

He had gone almost halfway before his horse stumbled and fell. Finished, windbroken, ruined, the horse rolled its eyes at him as Cross picked himself up and drew his revolver from the holster at his side. He put a single shot into the horse's head, holstered the gun, turned and started helplessly toward the disappearing plume of smoke.

He waited impatiently until the others caught up with him. Ned Murphy, who'd had the foresight to bring along a fresh, extra horse, handed him the reins.

Quickly, Cross unbuckled the cinch beneath the fallen horse and pulled the saddle off. He threw it up on the fresh horse and cinched it down. He mounted and raked the horse with his spurs.

Once more he thundered away toward home, believing it would no longer be a home but a dead place like that hollow where the bones of the buffalo lay bleaching in the sun. He only knew he had to see, to know, to be certain that what he believed was true. He had to know they all were dead because there was always some hope, some little hope that the Cheyenne, who loved children no matter what their race, had taken the children instead of killing them.

With maddening slowness the miles dropped away behind. Once again Morgan's spurs were bright with blood, his horse's neck flecked with foam. Once again the horse wheezed, his sides working like some gigantic bellows as he fought for air to keep going on.

Morgan saw the place while he was still a half mile away, topping a low crest and looking down into the wide, shallow valley of Calf Creek. The barn still stood, and the sod root cellar, and two or three sheds and the chicken house. All that had been burned was the house. And all that was left of the house was a black pile of ruins a couple of feet high that sent a thin plume of smoke straight up into the motionless air.

From here he could see the heat waves rising too, along with the smoke, distorting the shapes of things beyond the house. He squinted against the glare of the sun overhead, frantically searching for movements with his glance, all the while spurring recklessly and thundering ever closer to the place.

He heard the milch cow bawl in the barn, and saw a couple of white chickens scratching in the barn doorway, and he felt the breath sigh out of him and stared even more intently than before, half-expecting to see Jess come out of the barn, or the two little girls, or maybe even his wife. Perhaps, he thought, the Indians had not been here at all. Perhaps this was only an accident — a burned house and nothing more. He did not believe it was, but he prayed, his lips moving grayly and soundlessly.

With only another quick, fearful glance at the smoldering rubble of the house, he swung down from the horse and ran for the barn. "Jess! Hope! Mary!" he called, and then, because it was an admission to fail to call her name he shouted, "Nell! Nell! For God's sake, where are you all?"

He slowed and almost stopped just short of the barn because he was suddenly afraid of what he might find inside. Clenching his jaws tighter, and his fists, he plunged through the doorway into the cool shadow inside the place.

His breath, which he had unconsciously been holding, sighed slowly out. He turned his head and looked around.

Nothing. There was nothing here. No children. No wife. Only a couple more chickens scratching in the dry manure, only the cow that bawled at him reproachfully, her udder distended and tight as the skin covering of a drum. Her calf was gone.

It had to have happened last night, he thought. The cow had not been milked today. He ran back outside just as the others came thundering into the yard. He looked up at them and shook his head, not missing the way their glances went instantly to the embers of the house.

Frantically, now, he ran toward what was left of it. The heat was still terrible, too great for him to get close, too great for sifting through anything.

Chet Rittenhouse, young and brown, his yellow hair like an unruly shock of straw, called, "Hey! Take a look at the tracks!" and for the first time, Morgan Cross remembered to look.

Right in front of the house the ground was pounded by the unshod hoofs of several horses and there were moccasin tracks . . .

Overlying the tracks of Nellie's shoes. Overlying the smaller tracks of the little girls, the tracks of Jess's heavy work boots.

Ned Murphy dismounted beside him, his face red, cold fury blazing from his eyes. He ran to the barn, returned immediately carrying a fork. Ignoring the heat of the embers, he plunged into what had once been the kitchen, probing with the fork.

Len Rittenhouse and Chet plunged in

after him, seizing him by the arms and dragging him out. His boots were smoldering and theirs were too. They dragged him to the little pond just outside the corral, stepped into the water with him and then let him go. Len Rittenhouse said harshly, "Don't be a fool, Ned! Who's it going to help if you burn the soles of your feet off so's you can't even walk? You want to go after 'em? All right, go after 'em. But there's no use digging around in those ashes now. Whatever was in there when it burned is gone. You won't find anything. I recollect the time the Chavez place burned on Beaver Creek . . ."

Chet, who had been looking at Murphy's face, said, "Pa! Not now!"

Cross was sitting on a chopping block staring at what was left of the house. His face, his expression held an empty quality, and his eyes were almost blank.

He was seeing Jess, trying to hold that plow, his face twisted with concentration and stubbornness. He was seeing the little girls, dressed up like dolls for a trip to Dodge. He was seeing Nellie, her face framed by the white wedding veil . . .

It was all gone now. His family. The children, for whom he had stayed, enduring Nellie's refusals these last seven years, the house which his father had built so long ago.

It was gone, because of a handful of murdering, dirty redskins, taking out their hatred of the white race on a woman and three innocent children who had never hurt anyone, whom they had never even seen before.

Rittenhouse yelled suddenly, "I say we'd all better get back to our own places before the same thing happens there! I know I'm going back, just as damn fast as I can get there! Come on, Chet."

Gleason Calloway said, "Come on, boys. We'd better get for home too. There ain't nothin' more we can do around here." He rode to where Morgan sat and stared down at him. "We'd stay if there was anything we could do. But there ain't, Morg, and a thing like this kind of gives a man a turn."

Morgan didn't even look up. He seemed to be in a daze.

Calloway turned his horse and rode away. He glanced at the old wolfer, Gray. "You coming, Dave?"

The old man shook his head, his eyes bright in a face dark as mahogany and covered with a week's growth of graying whiskers. He said, "They kin burn my shack if they're a mind to. I reckon I'll stay here a spell. Might be Morg would want to track them bucks."

Calloway nodded. Rittenhouse and his son were already a couple of hundred yards away, in the direction they had come. Calloway touched his horse's sides lightly with his spurs and followed them.

Morgan Cross was left. And the wolfer, Gray. And Ned Murphy, who seemed almost as dazed as Morgan was. And Murphy's two half-grown sons.

Almost as though he had just waked up, Ned Murphy suddenly yelled, "What the hell are we waitin' for? Let's go after 'em!" His body was trembling. His voice quavered like a boy's. But there was nothing shaky about the cold determination in his eyes.

# CHAPTER ELEVEN

It was almost noon by the time Orvie Watts clawed his way up through the gray rim of sandstone rocks guarding the top of the flat butte he had seen earlier. The sun was hot, now, and sweat ran off his forehead and down both sides of his face. His eyes were red, bloodshot, his lips dry and cracked. There was dust caked on his unshaven face. His clothes were soaked with sweat and also covered with fine gray dust.

His head ached ferociously. Occasionally he would put a grimy hand up to touch the tomahawk wound. It had swelled considerably and was now a walnut-sized knot upon his forehead. It was caked with blood.

He stared from the butte top out across the wide, endless plain toward the south. From up here the land looked almost flat but he knew there were hollows in it, and ravines, and canyons and arroyos that could hide an army ten times the size of the group of three hundred fleeing Cheyenne.

White, puffy clouds drifted across the sky. Toward the west thunderheads were beginning to pile up, white and gigantic and beautiful, not yet turned gray with the threat of rain.

The sky itself was blue — a flawless, clear blue and the land beneath it was a dry, light shade of tan. Dry grass waved in the breeze, sometimes looking like the waves of a limitless, brownish sea.

There, in the distance, he could follow the valley of the North Fork of the Solomon River and beyond that, shrouded by the haze of distance, could see where the South Fork was. Beyond were the tracks of the Kansas Pacific Railroad, and farther still the Smoky Hill River and beyond that, Dodge. But Orvie Watts was looking southwestward now, away from Dodge toward the area where he knew the Cheyenne had to be.

He sat down and let his head sag forward to lie upon his folded arms resting upon his knees.

He lay back, wincing, squinting at the pain the movement caused. That damned Cheyenne tomahawk had probably split his skull. He might end up paralyzed. He might lie here and die.

He lay there miserably for the better part of an hour. The sun began to slide slowly down the sky. And then, Orvie Watts's body relaxed at last. His breathing became more regular. He slept.

Mannion dismounted from his horse. The man on the ground was staring at him, wildness in his eyes. Mannion looked at the corporal. "Is this him, Corporal?"

"Yes sir. This is him."

Delaney got up. He grinned at the lieutenant. "He sure came uncorked, didn't he, sir?"

Mannion squatted in front of Orvie Watts. The smell of the man was rank, a combination of the smell of bones, and sweat, and grease and dust. And mules too. Mannion's face did not reveal the fact that the smell was almost overpowering. He asked, "How do you feel now, Mr. Watts?"

"All right, I guess. My head still aches."

"You've probably got a concussion or a fractured skull. How did it happen anyway?"

"Tomahawk."

"Knocked you out and they thought you were dead. That's why they didn't kill you."

Watts shook his head gingerly. "No. They knew I was alive. They just ain't looking for any more trouble than they've already got. They won't kill anybody they don't have to kill."

"They killed your helper. We found his grave."

"He must of went for his gun. He likely

didn't give 'em no choice."

"You sound pretty sure. I'd say you were being mighty charitable for a man in your fix. You've lost your mules. Your harness is slashed and will have to be replaced. Your wagons might not even be there when you get back."

"I lived with these Indians, Lieutenant, years ago an' I ain't exactly charitable. I'll git back at 'em. I knew one of the bucks that jumped me back there."

"You knew him?" Robert Mannion's voice was skeptical.

"Yes. Lame Bear."

"Maybe that's why you weren't killed."

"No. I told you why, lieutenant. They ain't looking for trouble. They're trying to stay out of it. Lame Bear's got no reason to like me. He'd as soon kill me as anyone. Maybe he'd rather kill me than any other white."

Mannion studied him for several moments. Finally, he asked, "Do you think you'll be able to ride?"

"I can ride, Lieutenant." He wrinkled his nose and his face turned pale. Mannion smelled the smoke of a fire, and coffee boiling, and bacon too. "Smell of food make you sick?"

"Don't worry about me, Lieutenant."

112

# CHAPTER TWELVE

The Sappa was ahead, and the place of the killing three years ago, and still the Cheyenne eluded the troops, although they were said to be closing in from many sides. General Dodge was marching down the Sappa to intercept. Infantry and cavalry were coming down the Little Beaver, more coming down the Beaver itself toward the Republican.

The young men continued to bring in horses from their raiding, and sometimes mules like the bunch Lame Bear had brought in early this morning, mules that bore the marks of harness on them and faintly smelled of death and rotting flesh.

Willow still walked, having no horse to ride. She had no man to go get a horse for her, but she did not mind walking because she was young and strong and with long legs well fitted for it. She would not have ridden herself even if she had obtained a horse because there were still many not strong enough to walk who were walking anyway.

She carried the pale, small boy, who watched her always with his great, dark eyes that seemed too large for his wan and sunken face. Sometimes, when she grew tired, or when the boy fussed fitfully, she put him down and let him trot beside her so that he would be tired enough to sleep when night time came.

And always the young men galloped out, yelling and waving their rifles or lances in the air, as though this long trek north were some kind of children's game, to be played at and enjoyed, as though it were not deadly and perhaps the last game any of them would ever play.

Little Wolf cautioned them about violence against the whites, telling them only to take horses and cattle for food, but to let the white people live. Willow watched his face as he spoke, knowing he spoke from ritual, almost from habit, not believing his words would change anything the young men did, sure that many white people would be killed no matter what he said.

A young man, younger than Willow, who was named Spotted Horse, came running to her, perhaps because she was on the far flank of the moving band, and a little to the rear. "There are two horses in that draw you see over there. We can catch them and ride instead of walking but you will have to help me a little bit or they will get away."

She nodded, and put the boy down with

her bundles in a small washout behind a huge clump of yucca. She followed Spotted Horse at a steady, silent trot.

They entered a long shallow ravine, in the bottom of which was a dry wash about waist deep. Spotted Horse pointed excitedly to the tracks of two horses in the sandy bottom of the wash. "Sit down and rest for a while, and I will circle and drive the horses toward you. When you see them coming, you are to stand and let them see you, and that will stop them and perhaps turn them back in confusion toward me. If I can catch one of them, catching the other will be an easy thing."

He had a rope — not a rope braided from grass in the Indian way, the loop of which must be held open with a willow hoop, but a white man's rope, thin and strong and stiff enough to throw with the loop staying open as the rope sped through the air.

Willow nodded silently and crouched down in the little wash and stayed there motionless while Spotted Horse made a large, wide circle to the north before coming back again into the washout at the bottom of the draw.

It would be a good thing, Willow thought, if she could get a horse. No longer would she have to carry both her bundles and the boy. She could put them on the horse's back, and walk ahead, the lead rope in her hand. Her strength would then be sure to last until they reached the north country so far away.

Trembling slightly, she waited. The horses would be conning soon. When she stood up, she should do so silently so as not to frighten the horses too much. If they were too frightened they might bolt up out of the wash and out of the ravine instead of turning back the way they had just come, or stopping and milling in confusion the way Spotted Horse hoped they would.

She heard their hoofs upon the sandy bottom of the dry wash, not coming very hard but only at a trot. She looked toward the sounds, waiting, and when she saw them come into sight, stood up very slowly and carefully.

The horses saw her and stopped. They did not seem very frightened, having not yet caught her scent because the wind was blowing out of the south, crossways to the ravine. Motionless she stood there, waiting for them to turn and go back toward Spotted Horse, scarcely daring to breathe for fear they would plunge up out of the wash and run away over the hill before Spotted Horse could throw his rope at them.

One of the horses was a big black animal with hoofs as big as both of a man's hands placed together, a horse for working, she knew, for pulling a plow through the tough prairie sod. The other was a bay horse like that of the soldier chief Lewis who had been hurt south of here in the fight on Punished Woman Creek. Except that this bay horse was not as beautiful as Lewis's horse had been, or as young. He was old, and swaybacked, but he was fat and strong for all that and a fast horse was not needed by Willow but only a horse that was strong enough to carry her bundles and the boy.

A shift of wind apparently blew a faint scent of her to the two horses for they pricked their ears and their eyes rolled white. They whirled, acting like colts when the spring rain comes slanting out of the sky, and went back down the wash the way they had come. She ran up out of the ravine, trying for high ground from which she could see.

Reaching a small knoll, she caught a glimpse of the black and the bay, and thought she saw a flash of a rope in the air, although she could not be sure. Then she heard a shout, and ran toward the sound, knowing Spotted Horse had caught one of them.

She was laughing and elated, and saw Spotted Horse's young, laughing face turned toward her . . .

But suddenly the laughter was gone from his face and he shouted, "Willow! Get down! White men are coming over the ridge with guns!"

She dropped instantaneously, but knew she had been too late because she heard the slapping sound of a bullet striking earth beside her and after that the high whining sound as it ricocheted away into the air, and then the sharp bark of a rifle on the ridge.

Faintly came the sounds of shouting, and she rolled, and looked toward the sounds, and saw four mounted white men galloping straight toward her waving their guns in the air.

They were still more than two hundred yards away but plain enough for her to see clearly even though she did not see too clearly the expressions their faces wore.

Suddenly it was like it had been back there on the Sappa three years ago. It was like it had been at Sand Creek when she was but a child and the whites had come bursting into the tipi to slaughter her brother and sisters as if they had been animals. She seemed to smell the powder and the blood and the smoke of burning leather and flesh and clothing upon the pyre, and their yells were like the white men's yells on the Sappa and at Sand Creek long before.

She got up and ran toward the little dry wash at the bottom of the ravine and threw herself into it, rolling when she hit the sandy bottom. Guns were popping in volleys now, both rifles and revolvers, as all the white men opened up. The bay horse jumped up out of the dry wash and galloped away over the ridge, but Spotted Horse had his rope on the stocky black work horse and he held on even when the horse tried to get away. The horse was frightened, but not wild like a riding horse might have been and Spotted Horse was able to hold on to him. Lying in the bottom of the dry wash, he shoved his rifle ahead of him and pointed it at the approaching whites who still had only seen a woman, and an unarmed one at that.

He fired. Black smoke billowed out ahead of his rifle. The thunder of approaching hoofs stopped suddenly, and so did the triumphant yelling of the whites. Only one yell cut the silence, a thin, high yell of pain.

An exulting expression of savage joy touched Spotted Horse's face. Silently he lay there, behaving like a seasoned old Dog Soldier instead of like the young and untried warrior that he was. He carefully measured the powder to reload his old rifle and then poured the powder in and rammed it home with the ball, and after that looked to his flint to be sure it would fire the powder he had put into the pan.

The white cowboys had withdrawn, but they had left one of their numbers writhing on the ground with a streaming leg wound which he held with both hands while he shouted curses at them for leaving him. They dismounted at the top of the ridge, hiding their horses behind its crest, and crept back to throw themselves down where they could see the whole ravine They did not know how many Indians were down there, Willow realized. Had they known it was only a woman and a young warrior with a muzzle loading rifle and very little powder, they would have charged unhesitatingly and killed both of them immediately.

Spotted Horse turned his head and looked at Willow. "Get away. Crawl down this dry wash until you are far enough away and then get up and run. I will keep them here by shooting at them when they try to get the wounded man away."

She looked at him, understanding that he did not think either of them had much chance, understanding too that he had accepted the idea he would die himself but did not see why both of them had to die.

She said, "No. I will stay and help you fight. With two of us . . ."

"And how will you fight them? With your hands? With your little butcher knife? They have the short guns they hold in one hand, the guns that shoot five times without reloading once. Can you fight those guns with your hands or with your knife?"

She studied him, seeing his extreme youth but remembering too how cool and steady he had been. She would have unhesitatingly given her own life to save his but she knew that was impossible. He would die and he should not die, one as clear-eyed and steady as this one was. He should live, and grow old and wise like Dull Knife and Little Wolf, and perhaps learn to lead the people in the ways of the whites.

But he was a man and a warrior and he knew she had the boy to carry north with her. He would not think of letting her stay in his place, would not even let her stay and help him fight.

Out there on the prairie the wounded cowboy suddenly shouted weakly to his friends, "Hey! There ain't but two of 'em! Come on down here! All they got is a muzzle loader and a knife!"

He had heard them talking and must understand the language of the Cheyenne. He had seen Spotted Horse reloading his gun and so knew how poor a gun it was. His first shouts had not been heard because they were weak and because there was the noise of more shooting up above, but if he kept on shouting he would eventually make them hear and they would come thundering down here to fill Spotted Horse with bullets from their guns.

Without thinking about it further, she leaped to her feet. With her knife clutched in her hand, she ran toward the wounded cowboy who now, belatedly, remembered that he had a gun.

He picked it up from the ground beside him and emptied it at her. It fired three times before the hammer clicked on an empty chamber and he threw it away from him.

Two of the bullets passed Willow's head, like angry bees. The third grazed the flesh of her upper arm, bringing instant numbness and an instant rush of warm bright blood.

But she had reached the cowboy now. She saw the stubble of whiskers upon his face. She saw the blueness of his eyes, eyes that suddenly had terror in them. She saw the stain of tobacco on his dry and cracking lips.

The faces of whites, seen close up, invariably reminded her of the faces of the ones who had come charging into the tipi at Sand Creek when she was a little girl. Without hesitating, she threw herself upon him, plunging the sharp knife home.

He writhed and struggled, and tried to choke her with his hands. He nearly succeeded but before he had, his hands relaxed and fell away from her throat.

Instantly Willow withdrew the knife and ran for the little dry wash again. Reaching it, she flung herself into it.

Spotted Horse was looking at her shoulder, so bright with blood. "You must go at once," he said. "You must save the boy."

She nodded. Silently she crept away down the wash, staying low and out of sight. When she was far enough away, she got up and ran, on swift and silent feet.

The sun was down now, and it was possible, she knew, that Spotted Horse would get away in the dark. He had a horse to ride, the big, black plow horse he had caught.

But back there, a white man had been killed. If Spotted Horse did not pay for it, someone else surely would. That was the way of the whites with the Indians.

She found the boy where she had left him before the last gray of dusk faded into the blackness of night. She knelt beside him and wrapped a strip of cloth around her upper arm, relieved to see that the bleeding had almost stopped. The arm ached ferociously but she paid no need to it. She lifted the boy up and carried him through the darkness toward the north, shaking her head angrily against the waves of weakness that washed over her.

The search for horses had turned out badly. She had a wound that would weaken her and slow her down. She had not succeeded in getting one of the horses for herself. She had gotten nothing but the wound.

Nor had Spotted Horse gained much, even if he got away with the big black work horse. A white man had been killed, and the whites would try to kill Indians for revenge. Any Indians. Wherever they might be found. But it had happened; it was done.

She clenched her jaws against the weakness and the pain and plodded on.

All through the night Willow plodded north, hurrying. She knew she must catch up with the others or risk being caught out here alone at daylight, without protection from the cowboys who were sure to be prowling the flanks of the main body of Cheyenne looking for stragglers they might kill easily.

An hour before dawn, she saw a few small fires ahead and to her left. She turned toward them, feeling great relief that she had made this much progress in spite of her wound. She would be safe if she could go on with only a little rest now before it got light again.

There would be food ahead, for herself and the boy, and the food would give her strength. Perhaps she could find a travois upon which the boy could ride today, with her bundles, and then all she would have to worry about would be herself.

She had almost reached the nearest fire when she heard a ponderous galloping of hoofs behind her. Turning her head she saw the big black that Spotted Horse had caught lumbering toward her with his great, awkward gait. Spotted Horse was bouncing up and down on the black's broad back, unable to grip the horse's huge barrel with his legs. He cried out to her when he recognized her. "Willow! See, I have escaped the white men and I have the black horse for you and the boy to ride."

"But the horse is yours. Now you will be able to join the other warriors when they go out raiding."

He slid down off the horse, holding the rope which he had fashioned into a kind of hackamore by looping it over the horse's nose. He took the boy from her arms and placed him astride the great, broad back. He lifted Willow similarly, bundles and all. He stood looking up at her.

There was a line of gray in the east, a thin, pale line that did not shed much light. And there were the stars overhead. She could see his face, but not the expression it wore. She could see his eyes, but could not tell what they might be revealing of his thoughts.

Yet she knew. Spotted Horse was looking at her the way young men look at young girls while they walk along a narrow path to the stream. He was younger than she, but he was looking at her as if they both were the same age . . .

She understood, suddenly, that it had not been chance that brought Spotted Horse to her with the suggestion that they catch the two horses yesterday. Spotted Horse had been following her, staying near, to protect her from any harm that might threaten her, to watch over her . . .

He led the horse away, toward the fires, his back strong and straight, his head high like a brave who has a woman and child of his own. And Willow closed her eyes because now that she did not have to walk and fight pain and weakness, both washed over her and threatened to steal away her consciousness.

They reached the fires and were surrounded by the people, exclaiming over the huge, strong horse, and sympathizing because of Willow's wound. One old woman stripped away her dress to expose it and treated it in the old way, with fine dust to stop the bleeding. After that, knowing the wound would heal, Willow gave the boy food and ate herself, sitting beside him, ever aware of Spotted Horse standing near and watching her.

Her feelings were confused but she knew the confusion was partly a result of pain and weariness. Spotted Horse must be three or four years younger than she, really only a boy even if he did have the height and breadth of a man, and the steadiness of an older man in his eyes.

Yet she was flattered too, feeling the warm flush of a young girl's confusion in her face and neck for all that she had borne and lost a son more than three years before. It was good to be wanted again by a man, to be found desirable. It was good to know there was someone to lean upon besides herself.

It might come to nothing, she told herself in an effort to avoid the exquisite pain of disappointment later. He might find another, younger girl and want her more than he wanted Willow now.

Let that be if it must. She had this warm feeling today, and she had him near to her, watching her, guarding her, and she had the black horse he had obtained for her at the risk of his life.

Most of all, most important of all, she was not alone. She raised her glance and smiled at him, then lowered her glance to the food again.

# CHAPTER THIRTEEN

Lieutenant Robert Mannion had seen them pass, watching from a high, flat butte with twenty-foot rims of gray sandstone. He squatted comfortably on the ground, staring out across the plain at the little groups plodding so patiently northward toward the Yellowstone more than a thousand miles away.

They were like an army of ants, Mannion thought, without any great strength or importance singly but enormously powerful in the aggregate.

# CHAPTER FOURTEEN

Morgan clenched his fists. He stared at the sky in the west, at the rolling grassland ahead, at the long, shallow valley of the Sappa dropping away eastward.

As the last light faded from the sky the wolfer stopped and they went about the small tasks of making camp. The two boys went out and gathered up armloads of dried buffalo chips for a fire. Murphy built the fire and poured water from his canteen into a blackened coffeepot into which he threw a handful of ground coffee from a sack. Gray put on a skillet and dropped some bacon into it, and afterward began mixing up biscuits which, when he was finished mixing them, he put into a dutch oven to bake.

Morgan Cross hobbled the horses, except for one which he picketed out at the end of a rope. When he had finished, he stood a little distance away from camp, staring at the tiny, winking light of the fire and at the forms of the men and the two boys squatting beside it comfortably.

He knew they might lose the trail they were following. He knew it was quite likely that they would. The trail would be lost in three hundred other trails. The four bucks responsible for the burning and murder back there would become unknown and faceless in that throng of migrating Indians. He would never know who they were and therefore would be cheated of his vengeance against them individually. This was the likelihood. This was practically the certainty.

His son, and his daughters, and Nellie would lie consumed in the ashes of their home unavenged. He felt suddenly cold, as though he had a raging fever and was suffering from a chill.

They would not remain unavenged! If the four bucks lost themselves in the anonymity of the throng, then he would take his vengeance against the throng, or against any Indian he got in his sights.

Scowling savagely, he stalked back to the fire where the others were. They looked at his face, then uneasily looked away.

# CHAPTER FIFTEEN

Ben Terborg stayed with Captain Rendelbrock's command only a few days. At the end of that time, dissatisfied with Rendelbrock's progress, he badgered the captain into giving him an escort and went in ahead. He knew it was pure luck that they blundered into Colonel Lewis's command out of Fort Dodge, but he was on hand at Punished Woman Creek and watched the battle from a high point of land.

Afterward, he accompanied Mauck as he pursued the fleeing Cheyenne north. And every day, now that they were traveling through settled land, new stories of Indian atrocities came to Ben Terborg's ears.

One morning, in the first light of dawn, they came upon a weeping woman hiding in a small gully, a woman who turned hysterical with relief when she saw the long columns of mounted men, of Infantry riding in wagons, of canvas-topped supply wagons, and cook wagons, and ambulances.

"If you had only come a day earlier!" was her cry as someone tried awkwardly to comfort her and keep her face turned away while troopers picked up the grisly remains of her men and wrapped them in blankets and buried them.

Later that same day they found the body of a cowboy, killed by a bunch of warriors stealing cattle. In the same raid a lone boy was shot, a boy who could have hurt no one because he did not even have a gun. His body was found a quarter mile from that of the cowboy.

Scouts brought in similar stories almost every day. A settler, plowing, had been shot down in cold blood as he ran to his dugout to defend his wife, who was there alone. She had fled, and his son had fled, and they had not been pursued, but the man lay dead on the plowed ground of his field staring sightlessly at the sky.

As the days fled past, Ben Terborg's eyes became a little more cold, his mouth a thinner line in his bony, craggy face. He was witnessing the agony of courageous people, men of peace who had come to this country to plow and raise food and make full, abundant use of the land. He saw the tear-streaked face of a young woman whose husband and son had been killed, and he saw the empty aloneness of an old woman whose husband of fifty years lay dead with a Cheyenne bullet in his head for no reason at all.

He heard a man cry out in agony. "I told 'em they could have anyting I had! I told 'em to help themselves! But they killed her anyway because she put up a fuss over them hackin' up our featherbed. Why'd they have to do it? Why? She never hurt them none! Neither her nor me ever hurt an Indian in our lives!"

Fairness, for animals like these? Fairness for such savages? The Cheyenne were killers, senseless, brutal murderers. They killed for pleasure, for pure joy. The Army must hurry and catch up with them.

Near the headwaters of the South Fork of the Soloman, a small cavalry detachment approached, escorting a lone civilian. The column halted momentarily. Terborg pushed his horse to the head of it curiously.

A lieutenant was in charge of the new arrivals. He saluted Mauck. "They're about twenty miles ahead of you, sir. Traveling fast."

Mauck turned his head and saw Terborg. He said, "Bob, this is Congressman Terborg from over in Colorado. Congressman, Lieutenant Robert Mannion."

Terborg kneed his horse within reach of the lieutenant and stuck out his hand. "A pleasure, Lieutenant. How do you happen

134

to be out here all alone?"

Mannion gripped his hand. "I've been scouting, sir, and warning settlers. My orders were to rejoin this command when that was done."

"You've seen these Indians?"

"Yes sir."

"I want to talk to you."

Mannion glanced questioningly at Mauck. Mauck said, "It's all right, Bob. Tell the Congressman anything he wants to know."

The column started into motion again, ponderously and slowly because of its size and length. The civilian who had come in with Mannion and who was obviously hurt, was put into an ambulance. Terborg reined his horse far enough to the right of the column to get out of the dust and noise, and Mannion accompanied him.

Terborg studied him with open curiosity. It was a frank and blunt appraisal and it brought a slight flush to Mannion's face. Finally Terborg grinned, and Mannion asked a trifle irritably, "Well sir, what have you decided about me?"

Terborg's grin widened. "I like you, Lieutenant."

"Thank you, sir." There was definite reserve in Mannion's voice.

"Which is a polite way of saying you don't

135

give a damn what I think." Terborg's eyes were mocking.

"Should I, sir?"

"Not especially." Terborg was silent a moment, watching Mannion's face. At last he said, "I'm sorry, Lieutenant. I shouldn't have used those tactics on you."

"What tactics, sir?"

"My congressional tactics, I guess you'd call 'em. A member of Congress has a certain . . . oh hell, position sounds pompous. What I mean is that a Congressman gets treated with deference wherever he goes. He's allowed to see only the things people want him to see and nothing else. He's told what they want him to be told. I've found that if you make people mad at you, they'll tell you everything. I guess that's what I was trying to do to you."

Mannion studied him carefully for a long time as though trying to evaluate him and the things he had said. At last a slight smile appeared on Mannion's face. He asked, "What would you like to know, Congressman?"

Terborg felt himself relax, and was amused at himself, at the tension that had built up in him.

He fired questions at Mannion with the rapidity of a Gatling gun. "How many Indians are there up there?"

"Close to three hundred, sir."

"Drop the sir. I'm only a Congressman. Call me Ben, or Terborg, or anything you want."

"Yes sir."

"How many bucks — fightin' men?"

Mannion's eyes were thoughtful. "I don't know exactly. Maybe fifty or sixty. If you count boys and older men that figure might double."

"Well mounted?"

"Hardly, sir. They only have what horses they've been able to steal. The older horses and the work horses are being used by the women and old men. I'd say maybe thirty of those bucks were well mounted."

"Have they wounded?"

Mannion nodded. "Wounded women, wounded men, wounded children."

"You sound like you felt sorry for the lousy murderers."

"I do. I sure as hell do. They . . ."

"Never mind. I know what you're going to say. But what about that wounded civilian you brought in with you? What about women and kids killed all along their route? We have a few of the survivors in ambulances, Lieutenant, taking them to the railroad. Talk to some of them, Lieutenant. Then tell me how sorry you are for the In-

137

dians." Terborg's face was flushed.

Mannion said, "The Cheyenne are doing something they believe they have the right to do. They're returning to their homeland on the Yellowstone, as they were told they could if they didn't like it in the south. They were not given food for the trip, nor transportation. They have been attacked by the Army on three occasions so far and will be attacked again. They need horses, and food, and blankets, and clothes. They need everything and they have no money to buy it with. They must take what they need. They must take the necessities they need to sustain them because every hand is against them. And when someone points a gun at them, what are they supposed to do? Stand idly by and be shot and killed?"

Mannion paused for breath. His face was more flushed than Terborg's had been, and his eyes blazed angrily. He went on, "You're angry, Congressman, because of what has been done to the settlers. You want to retaliate, to wipe the Indians out. But aren't they entitled to feel the same anger against the whites? Aren't they entitled to strike back too?"

Terborg looked startled at Mannion's show of feeling. Mannion said, in a calmer tone, "I'm sorry, Congressman, but I get worked up. Several days ago I buried a human skull up ahead there on Sappa Creek. It was the skull of a child — maybe seven or eight years old. The top of it was caved in, either by a bullet or a club. The body had been tossed on a pyre, along with dozens of other bodies, and burned along with the tipis and clothes and other things the Indians owned. Those people were attacked at dawn, Congressmen, without warning of any kind. They tried to surrender but were refused even that luxury. Women and children and men were killed indiscriminately. It was like a housewife wiping out a nest of mice. A few got away, but that wasn't the army's fault."

Terborg stared at him with confused surprise. "What's the answer, then?"

Mannion shrugged. "I don't know. But there has to be a simpler way than this. Why can't the Army let the Cheyenne go north to the Yellowstone? Wouldn't it be easier to escort them there than to fight them all the way? Wouldn't it be better to give them horses and food than to have them killing settlers and taking them? Isn't there a little piece of land in this great, powerful nation of ours where three hundred little people can live in peace?"

Terborg stared at him, having no answer for such a simple question as that.

# CHAPTER SIXTEEN

They met the first of the troopers under Mauck as the sun was dropping into the broad, golden plain to the west. Morgan Cross pulled his horse to a halt, staring at the strung-out columns of horse soldiers and canvas-topped wagons drawn by Army mules.

The troopers were halting now as shouted commands rolled down the line. Horses were unsaddled and taken to picket lines where they were fed hay and grain from wagons loaded high with feed. Fires were built and the smoke climbed in thin bluish pillars into the still September air. A trooper came to Morgan and Gray and saluted perfunctorily, more of a gesture than a salute. "Lieutenant Mannion would like you gentlemen to eat with him. Will you follow me?"

Morgan and Dave Gray dismounted and followed the trooper through the crowded bivouac area. At last they reached the place, on the far edge of the camp, where Mannion waited for them.

The lieutenant nodded and extended his hand to Cross. "Glad to see you, Mr. Cross. I hope you didn't have any trouble with the

Indians. Did you get the men together as you planned?"

Cross nodded sourly. "I got 'em together, Lieutenant, but it was too late. Time I got back to my place they'd burned the house and killed my family."

An expression of concern crossed Robert Mannion's face. It was a genuine; horrified concern and not merely a surface expression of sympathy. He said, "Mr. Cross, I didn't know. Is there anything I can do?"

Cross nodded. "There is. I want to go along with you until you catch those Cheyenne and whip the hell out of them. There's a chance they've got my little girls."

"Didn't you find . . ." Mannion stopped.

"I said the house was burned. They were inside it, or at least that's the way it looked. There weren't any tracks except those the redskins made."

Mannion nodded. "You may be right. I've heard that Indians sometimes take children and raise them as their own. Perhaps your little girls . . ."

"How about it, Lieutenant? Can we go along with you?"

"I'll see. But I shouldn't wonder, Mr. Cross. We have other refugees with us. I don't know how much further we'll be going, though. Our supplies aren't going to last."

141

# CHAPTER SEVENTEEN

It was a clear, dry fall in this high and empty plain; with golden grass reaching away as far as the eye could see; terminating at the horizon in sky as blue as the turquoise of the Navajo. Puffy clouds drifted in that nearly flawless sky, and the sun was hot and bright.

Dust arose from the moccasins of the people, and from their horses' hoofs and from the cloven hoofs of the cattle they drove along with them. The leaves were golden on the giant cottonwoods in the river valleys and along the little creeks. And sometimes in one of those little creek bottoms a steel-gray buck deer would jump to his feet and bound away, pursued by a dozen of the men nearest him. Later the men would come back with the fat, smooth, gray carcass slung across one of their horses' rumps. And the carcass would be turned over to the women where they camped that night, to skin and cut up and divide among themselves.

The wounds sustained back on Punished Woman Creek were beginning to heal now — those that would heal, but there were a few wounded ones, with shattered bones or with festering wounds, who grew weaker and thinner and more listless with each passing mile.

Willow sat on the great, broad back of the work horse that Spotted Horse had caught for her, with the boy before her, with Spotted Horse plodding patiently ahead, leading the horse as though she was his squaw and the boy his son. He was a good and patient man for all his youth she thought as she stared at his muscular back, and he wanted her, and the fact that he did put a warmth in her that had not been there for a long, long time. It is good to be wanted, and even if it came to nothing, even if he found a younger woman and took her as his wife, she would have had this much and would not forget it soon. Besides, there was no guarantee that any of them would reach the Yellowstone. Twice more there had been little skirmishes with the advance elements of Mauck's force, and another man lay dead and there were several fresh wounds from those skirmishes. Mauck was raging now, the scouts said and some of his officers were very angry too that they had failed to catch and engage the whole force of Cheyenne and stop them and defeat them and bring them back. But the Cheyenne were traveling light, carrying nothing they did not have to carry, and not resting much or sleeping long at night. Each day the Indians waited to camp until their scouts said the soldiers had camped, and each morning they were traveling long before the soldiers had broken camp and started in pursuit.

They did not talk of what was ahead, except that the northern Cheyenne sometimes told their brothers who belonged to the southern Cheyenne what that north country was like, with the grass long and thick, with the game plentiful and taken easily, with the tall mountains standing sentinel over their villages clustered along the banks of the clear and rushing streams.

Yet all of them knew what lay ahead. They still had not crossed the Republican, nor the Platte, which many of them called Geese River because of the great flocks of geese encountered there. And along the Platte ran the tracks of the great iron horse that could haul cars filled with soldiers, their horses and armaments and supplies hundreds of miles in a single day and night. When the Cheyenne reached the Platte they might well find thousands of soldiers dug in and waiting for them.

But they did not think of all that might happen, and contented themselves with taking each good, warm day as it came. They ate, and they breathed deeply of their new freedom, uncontaminated with the smells they had known in the south because the villages were too long in one place.

They were free, and living as Cheyennes were meant to live, nomads of the great, high plain, living off the game they found. Some of that game was wild, but most of the meat they took came from the white man's cattle. Even that was all right for it was but a fair exchange. Had not the white men killed the buffalo?

Thus they reasoned, and on they went, willing to die if death was what awaited them at the end of the trail. It was better to die this way, free and clean and proud than to waste away and die broken in body and spirit in the pest-hole to the south.

At White Tail Creek, they stopped and camped in a steep-walled canyon, and here two men from another band came in with news that the Sioux were surrounded by soldiers so that they could not give assistance to the Cheyenne.

This frightened many of the Cheyenne, for some of them had been counting heavily on assistance from the Sioux. But they held their faces stiff and kept pointing their eyes stubbornly toward the horizon to the north.

145

If the Sioux could not help them, then they would have to get along without the Sioux. Yet many of them could not help thinking of the battles in which the Cheyenne had fought side by side with their brothers — the Rosebud fight when Crook was turned back, and even at the Little Big Horn where Yellow Hair was killed.

But with this news, something more terrible than hunger and cold and the wounds caused by the white men's guns came into the Cheyenne camp. It was disunity. Across the evening fires Dull Knife and Little Wolf exchanged angry words, with Dull Knife saying bluntly that Little Wolf was a fool, that people were dying of weariness, and weakness, people who had not even been wounded in the fights that had gone before. And to make things worse, he said, Red Cloud's agency was closed to them. Even this place where they had been before they left to go south was closed to them.

The warriors formed behind their chiefs, taking sides in the arguing, until all the camp was split in two, until faces were turned cold as stone and eyes blazed angrily at brother Cheyennes across the fires, until all were divided by opinions as to what course was best.

Willow watched with a heavy heart. She

did not trouble her head with what was best for the Cheyenne. That was what the chiefs were for, to decide what the people should do. If every woman, and man, old and young, had a voice in what happened, then there would be three hundred voices shouting at each other over the council fires. No. It was better that the people accept the judgment of their chiefs. But when the chiefs argued and disagreed — ah that was a bad thing for which she had no answer.

"What would you have us do?" roared Little Wolf, still strong and lean as his namesake the coyote despite his fifty-seven years. "Surrender to the whites?"

"We should go to Red Cloud," said Dull Knife. "Only by going to Red Cloud can we be saved. Soon snow will fill the air and cover the grass. The bitter cold will be upon us and we have no tipis and not enough clothes to keep us warm. Our horses will weaken and die and soon after that we all will weaken and die. We should go to Red Cloud now, while there is still a chance."

"Going to Red Cloud is the same as giving up to the whites! You know Red Cloud's agency is surrounded by the soldiers of the whites."

But Dull Knife's face was cold as stone and Willow knew he would not change.

Nearly half the warriors had taken their places behind him.

Desperately, she searched the faces of those who had, looking for Spotted Horse. She did not know what she wanted to do, and was confused by the arguments of the chiefs. She knew how savage the winter cold could be, and how the people would suffer if they kept on toward the Yellowstone. But also she knew the vindictiveness of the white men, and their stubbornness. They would haul any Indians who surrendered back to the south country just to prove they could, and the trip would be made in the snow and winter cold just as the hard trip north would be.

Still, she knew that what Spotted Horse did, she would also do. Then she saw his face, flushed with anger, among those who stood behind Dull Knife.

She would go to Red Cloud, then, and if it be to capture then that would have to be. No one can see into the future in order to tell what was right. Little Wolf was a wise chief, but so was Dull Knife wise. Either might be right, or both, and every Cheyenne here at White Tail Creek must make his choice.

And so, in the night, Dull Knife and those who had chosen to follow him moved out, a little toward the west. Because they knew they were going to surrender to the soldiers, they left a gift for Little Wolf and those who stayed with him. They left a robe and upon it powder and lead and the few poor arms that they could spare.

And as though to hide their going, a thick fog came over the country during the early morning hours, turning the grass wet underfoot, making the bushes and the trees drip with the moisture that condensed from it.

Behind them, now, were two commands, those of Major Thornburgh and of Mauck. Thornburgh pursued the Indians under Dull Knife northwestward through the sandhills, pressing close, not even stopping to rest his horses or his men. His men must have been eating in the saddle while they kept coming on, because so close were they behind the Indians that they nearly ran down one or two of the stragglers.

It was decided that something must be done at once, to slow Thornburgh's pursuit. Otherwise he would overtake and surround them and if that happened they would all be killed. It would not be like surrendering at Red Cloud's agency, where thousands of angry, well-armed Sioux warriors would see to it there was no massacre, no killing of old ones and women and children.

So some of the young warriors were sent back, to make an attack on Thornburgh's ambulance, a loud attack that would pull Thornburgh's men together and make them stop for a little while.

They traveled in silent hopefulness that the attack would succeed and the soldiers stop long enough for them to escape. Dull Knife ordered that they disperse now, spread out and scatter like quail that have been surprised. Thus their many trails could be lost except the decoy trail the ambulance attackers were to leave for the Army scout to follow.

Almost, the people held their breaths waiting. Willow found herself alone in the thick blanket of fog, in a world that seemed unreal. Bushes and trees loomed out of the fog ahead of her, assuming weird and fanciful shapes. The boy began to whimper, either because he was afraid, or cold, and Willow leaped to the great horse's back behind him, holding him close against her body to warm him and calm his fear.

And then, suddenly, she heard a muffled popping of gunfire back there, followed by a louder, more authoritative popping from the soldier guns that held more powder and therefore made a louder noise. This went on for quite a while, long enough for Willow to travel almost a quarter mile. It died out, then, and she instantly knew why. Dull Knife's men had given almost all of their powder and ball to those of their brothers who went with Little Wolf, leaving it on a blanket on the ground. They had been left with only a little powder, and when that was gone they had been forced to draw away.

But now, the second phase of the plan would start. The warriors who had attacked the ambulance would withdraw, but not so fast but what Thornburgh's men could follow them. A decoy trail would be left, plain enough for even the white men to read, and here and there along this trail would be dropped small things such as the people might discard or lose along the way. Thus would Thornburgh's men be lured from the real trail, which was now so dim it would probably go unnoticed in the fog.

All that day, she traveled alone. Near noon, the fog grew thin and the sun shone through, putting a light without warmth on the dripping land. Willow stayed in the low ground so that she could not be seen from very far away. And always she kept on in the same direction, northwestward, toward Pine Ridge, where Red Cloud was. Spotted Horse would find her, if he was still alive . . .

Thought of him being dead made her whole body turn cold. It could not be! It must not be! Young as he was, he wanted her and she needed him. Who was to say she could not be a good wife to him, even if she was older and more experienced? Who could say that in truthfulness?

No, she thought. He would come. He would come and when this long flight was done, would take her as his wife. This thin, weak boy could grow strong again, and her life would be rich and meaningful once more. But first they must reach safety at Pine Ridge. And that was still many long, long miles away.

# CHAPTER EIGHTEEN

The pace was hard for the troopers in Mauck's command and with each day that the Cheyenne eluded him, he grew more grim of face, more hard of eye. But he continued to push his men, and push them, and push them still harder after that. They grumbled and they cursed their officers and non-coms, but mostly they cursed Mauck himself. "Let Thornburgh have them after they cross the Platte," the men growled sourly. "God damn 'em, they've run the guts clear out of us!"

Plainly Thornburgh was angry too, angry because he had been fooled into following the decoy trail. He abandoned the rest of his wagons just beyond this place, their trails going off in another direction, and plunged on, pushing the horses hard. He made fifty miles the first day, between camps, not even stopping long enough to rest the horses or let the men dismount. There were no places where little fires had been built to brew tea or coffee.

Mauck was jubilant, for he knew they were getting close. He exulted to Chapman,

"Amos, Thornburgh's burnin' their god-dam tails! We've found near a dozen worn-out Indian horses his men have shot, and some of their packs and a lot of fresh-killed meat. They wouldn't leave things like that behind if they weren't getting pressed pretty hard."

But then something happened that ended his jubilation. He met the cattlemen scouts that had brought Thornburgh this far, going back. They were a sullen bunch, no doubt having been tongue lashed by Thornburgh and his men. "Why the hell should we chase the bastards clear to the Yellowstone? Answer me that. What do we owe the government? Have they protected us from the Indians? Hell no, they ain't. Will they pay us for the cattle we lost to them damned Indians? Hah!"

Cross knew one of the men, one named Williams from up on the Republican well north of his Calf Creek ranch. The man rode over to him and stuck out his hand. "You going back, Morg?"

Cross shook his head. "They hit my place as they went through. Burnt the house. Killed my family. Except maybe for my little girls. I'm hopin' they didn't kill my little girls."

The man's face was stricken. "Oh God,

I'm sorry, Morg! Damn I'm sorry! If there's anything I can do . . ."

Morgan Cross numbly shook his head. "Ain't nothing now. Ain't nothing you can do."

"I'd go along with you, Morg, if it would help."

Again Morgan shook his head. The man rode south, along with the others who had guided Thornburgh's men.

On and on and on into the trackless sandhills they went, always following Thornburgh's trail but never catching him. And at last Mauck stopped. Frowning, he told his officers he was going back. There was no use losing men, and horses, and materiél in a campaign that could not succeed. "They're Crook's responsibility now," he said. "Let him campaign out of Fort Robinson. If we get caught up here by a winter storm . . . I could lose half of my command."

So the troops turned back, but when they did, they left a little core of civilians determined to go on. For personal reasons, they were determined to go on. There was Morgan Cross, who would never stop until he had looked at the face of every child the Indians had.

There was Orvie Watts, and there was

Terborg, the Congressman. There was Dave Gray, the old wolfer, who claimed to know every hill between here and the Yellowstone, as did Orvie Watts.

But Mauck didn't dare let them go alone. Not without some kind of escort, some kind of protection from wandering Indians. If he let a United States Congressman go off and get himself killed . . . all hell would break loose for sure. Even worse than it already had.

So he gave them Mannion, who volunteered to go. And he gave them Corporal Delaney and another grizzled old trooper named Deseret. He gave them good horses and a few pack mules to carry their supplies. He waved goodbye to them, not knowing if he would ever see them again. They might catch Thornburgh and had orders to try, but again they might not. This was not settled country like it was farther south.

They rode off, following Thornburgh's trail, seven men in all with three pack mules, well loaded with food and ammunition and water, for the land ahead was dry.

Seven men, five of them with a personal reason for wanting to go.

# CHAPTER NINETEEN

This was a country of great silences, its grassy hills like the choppy waves of some gigantic inland sea. Orvie Watts rode in the lead, with Dave Gray lounging up the rear. Both of them were very much alert, their eyes scanning the surrounding hills continuously. A thousand Indians could be hidden there on either side and less than a mile away, and never be seen until they rode screaming to the attack. But each hill crested showed only another empty draw, and beyond that another empty hill, and Thornburgh's trail going on, and on, and on.

Northward they went, the hills growing less numerous, and higher, and the valleys between them wider. Here there were lakes, sometimes nearly dry, just a small puddle out in the middle of a cracked mud flat smelling so bad the horses wouldn't drink and the men didn't dare. And here, one early morning as the sun reddened the eastern sky, they overtook Thornburgh's column in the process of breaking their overnight camp and going on.

Thornburgh's men were a sorry-looking

lot, thought Morgan Cross. Their rations were gone, their hardtack, their salt pork and beans. They were subsisting on game, and on a stray, stringy beef they had killed the day before after carefully reading its brand and recording it so that the owner could be paid by the government. And on berries they found along the way, picking them when they would halt to rest the horses.

All of them were drawn with weariness and short of temper, and bearded because there was neither water nor the will to shave. And all held another, strange expression in their eyes, frustration because they had been outwitted and outguessed by a bunch of naked savages, because they had been out-traveled and out-endured by a bunch of women, old people and underfed children. It did something to a trooper's pride to have to admit a thing like that.

That night they camped at the head of a long, steep canyon with a stream tumbling down it and Thornburgh decided this must be Snake Creek that emptied into the Niobrara a good distance below Fort Robinson. Thus it was shown on his maps.

Next morning a couple of couriers from Fort Robinson intercepted the head of his column going down Snake Creek. Newspapers from one end of the land to the other had already consigned the major and his troops to the same heroes' graves as those in which Custer and his troopers lay. And Carleton too, with all his men, for that was who Thornburgh had been following.

No, the couriers said, there were no Cheyenne on the Niobrara and it was assumed they had gone on, northward already toward the Yellowstone.

Following Colonel Carleton's trail, the couriers pushed on, and next day Carleton sent back mules loaded with supplies for Thornburgh's exhausted men.

Cross felt a growing frustration at the news that no Indians were on the Niobrara or at Fort Robinson, or even eastward at Pine Ridge. Soon, he thought, the winter would set in. Soon snow would drive south on the howling northern winds and the temperature would plummet to zero and below. It could happen at any time.

And if his two little girls were with the Indians . . . if they were still alive . . . they might die of the cold for surely the Indians would not deprive their own children of warmth to clothe two of the stolen children of the whites.

To hell with staying with these slow-moving troops, he thought. To hell with hamstringing himself with their lousy government red tape. The way they were going, the U.S. Army would probably never find the Indians. First there had been Rendelbrock, then Lewis and Mauck, then Thornburgh and now Carleton too. To say nothing of other commands closing on the Indians from north and south and east and west, and all failing to turn up a single redskinned Indian.

Come the first storm, they'd flounder around helplessly in the snow, bellyaching that they weren't equipped for a winter campaign, without snowshoes or winter clothes, without feed for their horses since wagons could not get through. But they wouldn't say anything about the half naked Cheyenne who must live off the country as they went, who had neither enough horses nor any feed for them that they could not paw out for themselves.

No, he thought, it was time to cut away alone, or perhaps with Gray and maybe with Orvie Watts who also had a personal reason for wanting to catch the Indians. Maybe he'd wish he hadn't when he caught the Cheyenne because maybe he'd be killed, but at least he had to try. This way he might wander around all winter and never see an Indian.

But he'd stay with the troopers as long as they made good time and were traveling in the right direction, north. He'd stay with them to the Niobrara and then he'd see.

That afternoon they reached the deep canyon of the Niobrara, aflame with the great yellow torches of the giant cottonwoods, smoldering along the banks with the red of the wild rose and the willow, turned sometimes yellow and sometimes brown for up here winter now was close at hand. The grass was long and dry, and the river itself ran deep and swift and clear. And over all hung the long, drifting layers of smoky haze from the grass fires that now appeared to be farther north.

But they found no Cheyenne Indians. They found no tracks. It was as though the Cheyenne had disappeared like smoke into the air.

# CHAPTER TWENTY

Morgan Cross, Dave Gray, and Orvie Watts waited only until morning at Fort Robinson. Then they rode out, saying they were returning south because they knew the Army would not permit them to leave unless they did say that. And ride south they did, up through the White River bluffs, out across the divide and back down into the valley of the Niobrara. There was only one way to scout for the Cheyenne, Cross had decided, and that was to scout the Niobrara bottom and try to find their crossing, which he knew they could not completely hide.

"First thing we got to do," said Orvie Watts, "is to figure out where they were headin' for."

And the others listened because Watts had lived with the Cheyenne and was most likely of all of them to know what the Cheyenne might do.

They rode slowly down the Niobrara canyon, spread out, keeping to whatever cover there was not only to avoid discovery by the Indians but also discovery by any Army scouts that might be prowling around. That night they made camp in a narrow little canyon leading south from the Niobrara; keeping their fire small so that the smoke would not be visible from the plain above.

The afternoon of the second day they reached the place where the council had been held, wondering if the Sioux might not have wiped out all trails ahead of them. But the Sioux trail left the river bottom almost immediately, heading straight back north toward Pine Ridge.

They camped again that night, hiding themselves as before in a little canyon leading south from the Niobrara bottoms. And again, the following day, went on, but now in virgin territory as far as they were concerned and even beyond the place Carleton's scouts had been.

# CHAPTER TWENTY-ONE

Straight north they went now, with Willow and the boy riding and with Spotted Horse leading. Straight north, to camp that night with half a dozen others in a little canyon where the timber was tall and straight and fragrant.

The wind stirred ominously in the north that night and came sighing down the canyon through the tall straight pines. The air chilled and the boy burrowed against Willow shifting and turning and curling up like a hibernating animal making its winter nest. But when morning came there was still no snow in the air or upon the ground.

North again, the Pine Ridge drawing close ahead of them. North, to a camp in another canyon, this time with all the people who had come this way together with Dull Knife and the other, lesser chiefs. All together now, they made this camp on a small, narrow stream and waited while emissaries were sent to Red Cloud at Pine Ridge.

The emissaries dressed themselves in the best of the ragged finery they had left, wearing feathered headdresses that had been carefully put away all during the long trip north. From out of other packs came the few poor gifts they would take Red Cloud, and they rode the best horses among all those remaining to them.

But what they found was not encouraging. The few new buildings that had been built at Pine Ridge were surrounded by thousands of white soldier tents. They stayed back in the timber and sent signals to the Sioux and when a few of the Sioux finally came in response to the signals they said Red Cloud was a virtual prisoner, even with a soldier chief living in his lodge to spy on him. Red Cloud could do nothing to help, they said, so the Cheyenne took off their finery and slipped down unnoticed into the Sioux villages to see this for themselves.

And some of them returned to the little canyon where Dull Knife's people were, saying that Red Cloud was indeed surrounded and could do nothing. He had asked the soldier chiefs to let the Cheyenne come and live with his people but had been refused. The soldiers said all the Cheyenne must be surrendered so that they could be sent back south.

So Dull Knife and his headmen sat staring into the tiny fires, their features sagging, their eyes filled with defeat and hopelessness. They had separated from Little Wolf in the firm belief that the great Red Cloud, who feared no white man, would take them in and protect them from the whites. Now they knew this could not be. Red Cloud was afraid of the whites in his heart, for all the strong arrogance he showed in his face and in his words. He advised the Cheyenne to give up to the whites, and be fed. "And be sent back to the south country!" Dull Knife said bitterly. "Be sent back south to die!"

He stared into the fire, anger replacing the hopelessness in his eyes. "Never!" he said angrily. "Never!"

So they prepared to leave again, to continue north in spite of the fact that much time had been wasted here, much time of good weather so that now the winter storms were threatening. Yet they waited still another day because some of the men who had gone to talk to the Sioux were still with them there and had not returned.

At last they could wait no longer even for the return of these few, and so they gathered their possessions and started north again. Dirty gray storm clouds scudded south, sometimes wisping and shredding along the top of some lone, high ridge. A few flakes of snow stung the faces of the fleeing ones, turned bitter with discouragement. The storm had been threatening for days and now it had come but they must travel north in it anyway, no matter how they suffered from damp and from the cold.

Yet they knew the storm was not all bad. It would hide them as they fought through it toward the north. It would cover their trail almost immediately so that the whites could not find or follow them.

Could not find or follow them? Why, then, had they gone scarcely a dozen miles before they heard the muffled voice of a bugle following? Why, then, did soldiers in hundreds come galloping out of the snow, pursuing them?

The three whites Willow had encountered had certainly returned to Fort Robinson. But there had not been time, Willow knew, for soldiers summoned from Fort Robinson to ride to the Niobrara and follow her trail from there. Besides, snow would have hidden her trail and the other trails. No. The soldiers had to have found them another way.

Huddled together in the middle of the canyon, the people waited helplessly. They had few guns and no ammunition for them. They could not fight.

Besides, the heart was gone from them for

they knew they had been betrayed. By their friends, the Sioux, by their relatives at Red Cloud's agency. Or worse, by their own warrior men still with the Sioux at Pine Ridge, their own, who had not returned.

# CHAPTER TWENTY-TWO

Now the soldiers came up all around, the Sioux scouts first, American Horse who was related to the Cheyenne, and Two Lance and the others, and Joe Larrabee, the half-breed interpreter who knew the white man's language and also that of the Sioux and the Cheyenne.

The soldier chiefs wore long buffalo coats and high black boots and fur hats and great gauntleted gloves. Captain Johnson was in command and he looked at the pitiful people huddled here while the snow crusted his face, hiding the expression it wore. But his voice had no harshness or cruelty in it as he said through the interpreter, "I am glad I have found you. We will feed you and give you shelter from the storm."

Dull Knife shook his head stubbornly. "We have come a long ways and are going now to Spotted Tail of the Sioux, far from here where we will not bother you. We are not going back south for we were dying there. We are going to Spotted Tail."

Again Johnson offered them food and shelter, but he said nothing about not sending them south, about letting them stay here with the Sioux. When Dull Knife and his headmen continued to stubbornly shake their heads, he turned his head and issued orders to a sergeant standing close to him. This man raised his voice and shouted, and the troops closed in around the helpless Indians, their guns held ready in heavily mittened hands.

Willow huddled in the middle of the valley with the others. The boy she held close against her body now, a robe wrapped around both of them so that her own body's heat would keep him warm. Her head was encrusted with snow. She thought at least one of her feet was frozen, because it had no feeling in it at all. The other was cold and pained her fearfully, but she gave no sign of it.

In front of her stood Spotted Horse, his half-frozen hand on the knife at his waist. He would die for her if one of the soldiers threatened her, she realized, and in spite of her misery felt a warming of her thoughts.

Now Johnson roared at Dull Knife angrily in a way that frightened Willow and the others, who knelt, trying to huddle even closer to the ground to avoid the bullets they knew would now spray over them. But the anger of Johnson did not mean he would order his men to shoot. It only meant he was afraid — afraid that he might be forced to give such an order to his men. Or that in spite of him a battle would break out here between the helpless Indians and his well-armed men, a battle that could be nothing but a slaughter of the Indians.

Still Dull Knife repeated stubbornly that they would go to Spotted Tail, his voice low and snatched away on the howling wind. Johnson and his lesser soldier chiefs shook their heads, hearing the death songs begin down there in the valley as the people prepared themselves to die. The words of the songs were snatched away by the wind, but the mournful tones came through to the soldiers between gusts of it, in a minor key.

Again Johnson roared at the chiefs, telling them what would happen if they did not give up. At last Wild Hog and Dull Knife said reluctantly that they would ask the others. They returned to them briefly, afterward coming back to say sadly that they would go with Johnson and his men.

So back now they went, trudging sorrowfully along in the driving, deepening snow and the bitter cold. Back to the soldier camp farther along Chadron Creek where a huge, roaring bonfire had been built to warm the freezing Indians. Hardtack, bacon, coffee and sugar were given them in huge quantities by sober-faced troopers who sometimes blinked their eyes rapidly when they saw the swollen, frozen hands and feet of the Indians, or a dead child in a mother's arms, or an old one who had not even enough strength left to eat.

They built brush shelters against the cold, their open sides facing the huge bonfire, their backs to the dark and cold. And the night wind howled steadily, drifting snow high against the shelters, sometimes drifting it on over the sleeping Indians.

All night, the guards of the whites paced back and forth, slapping their mittened hands one against the other to keep them warm, stamping against the cold and sometimes calling into the night, "Halt! Who goes there? Advance and be recognized."

Willow slept at the front of a brush shelter Spotted Horse had built for her, the boy snuggled close. Behind, toward the rear of the shelter slept Spotted Horse, wrapped in a ragged, nearly hairless robe, but sleeping and apparently warm enough.

There had been a time, she thought, when people who saw him sleeping there would have smiled and talked among themselves. But not tonight.

At dawn there was a little trouble at the

172

edge of the camp and after that Captain Johnson sent for Dull Knife and ordered him to surrender his horses and his arms. Plainly Johnson feared that in spite of their condition the Cheyenne might get away again. He had heard of their incredible march from Fort Reno in Indian Territory. He had talked to some of Thornburgh's men and knew the ghostly way the Indians had of disappearing into nothingness. It would not be hard for them to disappear here, he thought, with snow drifting over tracks but short minutes after they were made.

And the Indians, as was their way, made a parley of the demand rather than dumbly accept it and surrender their horses and their arms. Cross-legged they sat around the fire and brought up the killings on Sappa Creek three years ago and they brought up Custer's killing of peaceful Cheyenne on the Washita a long time before, and the killing of other Cheyenne on Sand Creek even before that. And while they talked, down in the howling wind the Cheyenne women and men and children clustered very close together, passing the guns from the men to the women, who hid them underneath their clothing where they knew the white men would not look.

Spotted Horse gave his rifle to Willow, who took it apart, tying the two pieces, barrel and receiver, and stock, together with a rawhide thong which she then hung around her neck.

Cold as ice the gun hung against her naked skin, but gradually it warmed up from contact with her body until it became tolerable.

But now, Johnson seemed to understand what was being done. He ordered his men in close, separating the Indians, and making them file past him so that his men could look at them. Meanwhile the horses, some of the weaker ones, were brought forth.

Weapons were laid down upon the blanket, a few old, worn-out weapons but how were the soldier chiefs to know they were not all the Indians had? Bows and quivers of arrows, and stone tomahawks and maybe an iron one or two, and a lance, dull and perhaps crooked in the shaft, and here and there a rusty, worn-out knife.

Half a dozen guns, perhaps, all ones that would not shoot or guns for which there were no cartridges. Johnson let his men take the bows and arrows, the tomahawks and knives for souvenirs and then the Indians were counted by some of the Sioux scouts. There were a hundred and forty-nine in all, forty-six of which were men, the others women and children. They had a hundred and thirty-one horses and nine mules, and all these were taken away, driven south along Chadron Creek in the teeth of the howling wind.

They remained here yet another night, sleeping as before in the brush shelters facing the fire but without any longer any hope. Their horses were gone, and most of their weapons except for a few guns they had concealed. They had no food; they could not get away. They could only wait. From the past they knew that soon more soldiers would come. A new soldier chief would probably replace Captain Johnson in command. He would make demands that even the dwindling pride and helplessness of the Cheyenne could not accept. And then it would begin. Soldiers would ring the camp, their rifles threatening. Gatling guns would poke their evil snouts toward the people and perhaps even a howitzer or two would be readied, men standing at the breech waiting for the command to fire.

This happened, as they had known it would. During the night Colonel Carleton joined Johnson and his men and gave the order that in the morning the Cheyenne men were to be tied like animals and marched back to Fort Robinson if they still refused to go willingly.

The Cheyenne were told that there were wagons here for them to put their goods into, wagons in which they could ride back to Fort Robinson. And again they made a talk of this, a parley, to delay, to get more time for making this decision, so hard for them.

A simple decision, really, a choice between but two things. Surrender. Climb upon the wagons drawn by the strong black Army mules and go back to Fort Robinson and ultimately to the stinking hot land of the south, or break away, scattering like quail in the blizzard to die singly and alone or be hunted down and shot separately by the soldiers and the half-breed scouts.

A choice between all dying now and all dying later and more slowly than here. Not much choice, Willow realized, but it was not her decision to make. She was only a woman, with no family and no one to speak for her. She would do what the chiefs said, for she knew they were far wiser than she.

Yet she also understood that even this wisdom could not help them now. This was a decision not to be made with the mind but with the heart. Was it not better to die now with honor than to surrender and die dishonored later in the south?

This was what the people would have decided, she thought, if it had been given them to decide. It was not. The chiefs were the ones to decide. Dull Knife would decide.

"Hurry," Carleton said. "Hurry," wanting to get back to Fort Robinson and have this over with. But Dull Knife told him steadily, "You can say hurry but it is only this little battle you decide. We decide for the Cheyenne people, for all the generations to come, for all those yet unborn." And Carleton, for all his impatience, looked ashamed and was silent afterward for a while.

But the talk went on, the Colonel and the Captain insisting that the Indians go to Fort Robinson, or to Camp Sheridan and then to Fort Robinson, the Indians shaking their heads stubbornly and saying that Fort Robinson was just a step closer to the south. Or saying that as soon as they started to move toward Fort Robinson, and were strung out upon the trail, they would be shot by the soldiers.

Impatience showed in Carleton's face. He was cold and his men were cold and he was not getting anywhere. At last he said, "There will be no more food until we get to Fort Robinson. Nothing more until Fort Robinson."

Down in the Indian camp that night,

Willow laid the boy, snugly wrapped in the all but hairless robe, in a sheltered spot. Then she went to help the others with the work.

Little fires were built, low fires but long, to thaw the ground, and fed sparingly until that was done. When the ground was partly thawed, the fires were scraped away, and digging started in the muddy ground.

Slowly, holes were dug, rifle pits facing the soldiers over there. The earth that was scraped out of them was pushed up in front as breastworks against the bullets of the whites. The few guns left were brought out from beneath the women's clothing, and put together and loaded and made ready.

When the pits were dug and the earth breastworks thrown up, they cut down trees, and cut their branches off and dragged them to the breastworks where they piled them up on top.

But the Indians were not the only ones who were busy this night. More soldiers came from Fort Robinson to reinforce the whites. And more Gatling guns, and more cannon, loaded with grapeshot the way they had been at Sand Creek so long before, and some with great balls that would explode in the Cheyenne rifle pits, killing all the people there.

The morning came, the Indians still sleepless and near exhaustion from working all through the night. And in the first gray of dawn, Carleton sent for the headmen, for Dull Knife, for Left Hand, for Wild Hog. He showed them the cannon and the reinforcements and the Gatling guns. He told them they had but one hour by his watch to start for Fort Robinson. When that hour was up, he would give the order for his cannon to shoot.

Still Dull Knife talked for concessions, for promises that they would not be sent south, but Carleton shook his head. He could make no promises; he had not the authority. He could only bring the Cheyenne in.

Back to the people, the headmen went. Back, to give them a voice in their own destiny. But while they were talking a soldier courier came from Pine Ridge with news that food was scarce there too, that rations had not been sent, or if they had, they were late in arriving. This, decided Dull Knife, must be the reason Red Cloud had been unable to take them in. He had not enough food for his own.

It decided him, this hunger at Pine Ridge. He returned to the soldiers, to say sadly that they would go to Fort Robinson. If food was short in Red Cloud's camp it would be equally short in the camp of Spotted Tail. Spotted Tail would welcome them no more eagerly than Red Cloud had.

# CHAPTER TWENTY-THREE

Up out of the rifle pits the Cheyenne came, muddy, ragged, crippled and emaciated, some with hands and feet turning almost black from the freezing. Willow, whose frozen foot was like fire as it thawed, limped along carrying the boy who seemed almost lifeless now even though his heart still beat and breath still sighed in and out of him. Beside her stayed Spotted Horse, watching her face almost all the time, looking down sometimes at her frozen foot and worrying, though there was nothing he could do to help.

Fearfully they stumbled toward the wagons, not trusting the soldiers of the whites, remembering all the things that had happened to them at the hands of white soldiers in the past. Again Spotted Horse's rifle was slung in two pieces around Willow's neck, lying against her nakedness beneath her clothes.

A soldier, an oldster with his beard hoary with frozen breath, put out a hand to help her into the wagon, but she shrank from him, not looking closely enough to see the pain of compassion in his eyes. Half a dozen others, seeing her shrink away, turned and tried to run, but were stopped by the wall of soldiers surrounding them.

Spotted Horse walked beside the wagon where Willow was, limping a little on his own frost-bitten feet, looking up often to meet her glance with his own. The huge black horse had been taken away but she knew she would always remember that great animal whenever she looked at Spotted Horse.

Ahead rode Carleton and his troops, horses pulling the cannon, howitzers, and Gatling guns. Behind came the wagons carrying the Cheyenne, and other supply wagons and ambulances, and on both sides and in the rear were Captain Johnson's troops, given this place because they had been the ones to discover and capture the Cheyenne.

After a while the snow slackened and stopped, and the sky lifted, though it still stayed gray. The temperature plummeted, and the snow squeaked as the iron wagon tires rolled over it and the Indians were careful to touch nothing made of iron.

Here, where he could be seen by all, Wild Hog climbed upon the tailgate of a wagon, standing tall, ragged, emaciated and powerful, his eyes gleaming with an almost fanatical light.

He said that the white men lied, that they always lied, that their promises to hurt no one were also lies. He told of all the broken promises of the whites, and told them promises made now would be broken too.

He offered them immortality at the next canyon, an everlasting place in the memory of all Cheyenne, indeed in the memory of all Indians, if they would leap from the wagons and attack the soldiers with the weapons still hidden in their women's clothes.

But Johnson saw him and sent some of his men plunging ahead through the drifts for more soldiers and they came before the wagons reached the next canyon and leveled their cocked rifles at the Indian men, waving them back, forcing them away from the wagons where the women and old ones were.

So the revolt died before it was born and the column wound stubbornly onward, horses lunging ahead, abreast, to break a trail through the deep and drifting snow. They wore out quickly doing this, and so were replaced by fresh horses and fresh men, and replaced again later on. In the last, deep gray light of day, the column of troops, walking now to keep from freezing in their saddles in the bitter cold, came down into the White River valley and Fort Robinson, yelling out and laughing with relief and making soldier jokes that the Indians did not understand. Out of the cutler's store came Orvie Watts, and Morgan Cross, and Dave Gray, the air biting their nostrils as they breathed and great clouds of frozen breath issuing from their noses and their mouths. They stared at the column as it halted, at the huddled, beaten Indians, at the soldiers looking, in their great warm coats like bears lumbering along in the half light of dusk.

Cross said, "Holy Christ, if my kids *are* with them they'll be frozen stiff." There was an excitement in his voice now as he watched the Indians herded toward a long barracks with lights and a fire inside. "Tell 'em to drop their packs and bundles in a line outside the door," Johnson told the interpreter. "We'll search 'em for weapons and then they'll be returned."

The interpreter translated and the Indians froze motionless again, and again the soldiers stepped in close, ready with rifles showing naked bayonets. Resignedly the Indians put their bundles down in the snow, knowing there were things in them that would incriminate and make the white men hate them even more than they already hated them. In those packs were trinkets taken down in Kansas from the houses raided by the young men. They were things that could be identified, things that would have special meaning to special whites, some things even with names engraved in them.

But there was no help for it now. The bayonets were too close, too sharp, and the Indians too exhausted from the cold and the long march north. Already nearly a thousand miles lay behind, but now it seemed as if it all had been in vain, the effort wasted along with the lives of those who had died along the way.

They'd be sent back down the same long thousand miles to the same stinking, unhealthy place from which they'd come. They were defeated; they had lost.

It was a relief to step into the barracks though, a relief for every one of them. On a stove in the barracks there was coffee cooking, filling the air with its smell. And because of the warmth a few of the older and weaker ones wept briefly, stopping soon because of the shame of thus showing their feelings to the whites.

Cross came to the barracks door, but was stopped by two soldiers guarding it. He brushed them aside with an impatient sweep of his arm and burst into the barracks to stare coldly at the Indians there.

Lamps hung from the rafters, giving him light to see many things he had not been able to see before — the pitiful condition of these people, their frozen, rag-wrapped feet, their drawn faces, the bloody bandages wrapped around their wounds.

There was a smell here too, almost like the smell of a rain-wet dog, but besides that smell there were others — of campfire smoke — and grease — and the wild smell of the pine forest in which they had been caught.

He swept the room with his glance, letting it rest briefly on each of the hundred and forty-seven here, but more closely on the children about the size and age of his own lost two. He saw Willow, recognized her instantly as the woman they had caught a week ago in the Niobrara bottom, afterward returning to Fort Robinson to tell Carleton about the trails they had found going north. If she recognized him she gave no sign of it, regarding him as coldly as did all the other Indians.

Outside, behind him, he heard one of the soldiers yelling for the Corporal of the Guard to come and eject him from the place but he paid no heed, telling himself grimly that he would not be ejected until he had looked at every one of the children here.

Long before he had finished, he felt a kind of coldness begin to grow in his chest. They weren't here. He wasn't going to find them here. Less than half of the Indians who had escaped Fort Reno were in this room with him and his two lost children were not among those here.

He had looked at every child in the room, at every single one that was even close in age and size to either of his own lost two. He heard soldiers coming in the door behind him to take him out and started to turn to go with them . . .

Suddenly he saw something he had not seen before. It was a patchwork quilt, one he recognized, one that had unmistakably come from the upstairs bedroom of his own Calf Creek house.

He could not be mistaken. He had watched Nellie make that quilt with her own fingers, meticulously stitching each square in place. He recognized the materials as having been scraps from dresses Nellie had made for the two little girls and scraps from dresses she had made for herself.

It was so dirty as to be almost unrecognizable, and that was why his eyes had passed over it the first time he had looked at it. Now, suddenly, all his self control was gone. All caution, all concern for his own safety disappeared with it. He lunged forward, forgetting that he had a gun, forgetting everything but the hunger to get his hands on that murdering redskin's throat.

He reached the man, hearing the shout that went up behind him from the soldiers charging into the room. His body weight bore the Indian back, a brave near to twenty, Cross guessed in the hasty glance he got. Then his hands had closed around the Indian's throat and the two were thrashing around on the floor, rolling against the others' feet.

A voice bellowed, "Hold it! Stay out of it!" but they were English words and could not be understood. More easily understood by the Indians was the rifle shot that filled the room with its roaring sound, the black-powder-smoke billowing out in a great blue cloud making the people nearby choke and cough.

The Indian's face was turning blue but Cross's fingers were inexorable, tightening, tightening. The Indian thrashed, whipping his body back and forth, trying to break Cross's hold, meanwhile trying to get at his knife but failing because the folds of the blanket covered it.

Dimly Cross heard the shouting of the soldiers, dimly felt them crowding around him, their hands pulling at him, trying to tear him away from the dying brave.

Something slammed against the side of his head, something hard and solid that put a brassy taste into his mouth and made his senses fade. He felt his fingers loosening on the Indian's throat, and felt himself being forcibly dragged away. There was more yelling, both from the Cheyenne and the soldiers, and there was movement as he was half dragged, half carried back out of the barracks into the cold and snow outside.

He began to struggle and fight them now, and was dragged into the cutler's store. Released, he stood, swaying with dizziness, while two soldiers put their backs to the door facing him so that he could not get out again.

A lieutenant was there with him, not Mannion but another one who was stationed here. He said coldly, "What was that all about, Mr. Cross?"

"That quilt . . . the one that murderin' thief was wearing . . . my wife made it. He's the one that burned my house and killed my family!"

"You can't be sure of that. Just because . . ."

"It's enough for me." He said it with angry surliness, his head throbbing almost unbearably from the blow of the rifle stock. His vision blurred and bright lights swam before his eyes.

The lieutenant said, "Mr. Cross, this is an Army post. You are here as a guest. If there is any repetition of tonight's attack . . . you will be asked to leave. Is that clear, Mr. Cross?"

"It's clear enough. But don't count on makin' it stick."

# CHAPTER TWENTY-FOUR

There were newspapermen at Fort Robinson, and some civilians, with more coming in every day claiming horses and filing claims for cattle killed and property destroyed. And there was Ben Terborg, the Colorado Congressman, who had watched the Indians brought in on the wagons in the storm, silent in their suffering, wrapped so in their ragged blankets and robes that only their eyes and their clouds of steamy breath were visible.

The newspapermen wanted stories and as soon as they were permitted to, they interviewed the Indians, and the Sioux scouts who had helped find them and bring them in, and the officers too, Colonel Carleton and Captain Johnson, trying to find out what the Army intended to do with the captured Indians.

Some were to be sent away, Terborg learned, when it was discovered who among them had done the killings back in Kansas to the south. The Governor of Kansas was demanding in the newspapers that the guilty Indians be returned so that they could be tried and hanged. Terborg noted that he said "tried and hanged," not just "tried," and the distinction between the two expressions did not escape him.

Where the others were, those under Little Wolf, no one knew. At least none of the soldiers knew. But one day two Cheyenne were brought in, scouts from Little Wolf's band, who had come here to see Dull Knife and had been caught trying to get to him. When questioned, their faces became like stone and they would not tell where Little Wolf had gone.

Terborg accompanied the post surgeon that first morning when he went into the barracks to examine the Indians. He did not know exactly what he expected or what he had prepared himself to see. Here were the Indians who had kept the telegraph wires busy from one end of the continent to the other. Here were the ones, this handful, who had made fools of the mighty United States Army and its generals. Here, too, were the ones who had killed forty whites in Kansas, among these the family of Morgan Cross and the mute helper of Orvie Watts.

He looked at them in this barracks, clad in rags, blankets and clothes they had stolen from the whites. He looked at their wounds, at their bloody bandages, at their swollen and frozen feet and hands. He looked at their impassive faces that endured the pain without sound or complaint, and he looked at the great, dark eyes of their children, at the pale, emaciated faces, the bony thin arms and legs and the swollen, protruding bellies.

Indeed the surgeon said he did not see why any of them were still alive. But they were not beaten yet. There was hostility and stubbornness in their eyes as they looked at the surgeon and his helpers. But there was a promise too. These people, Terborg realized with a shock, had not given up. They didn't know they were beaten. Perhaps they wouldn't know it until they all were dead.

The surgeon worked, his eyes narrowed as though the pain of the Cheyenne was his own personal pain. Yet they endured without complaint the tending of wounds that made Terborg's stomach churn just to look at them.

And even while the surgeon worked, the cooks came, carrying great kettles filled with steaming meat and potato and carrot stew. They brought more coffee too, and bread, and great jars of jam and molasses. They brought tin plates and cups, and the Cheyenne made a line down the barracks and back again, and accepted the food silently the way they had seen the soldiers do.

Some of the Sioux scouts also came and joined their friends and relatives, to whom they had led the soldiers but short days ago. Terborg frowned, trying to understand the Cheyenne lack of animosity. The scouts had taken pay, and trinkets and praise to betray their friends yet there seemed to be neither animosity in the hearts of the betrayed nor guilt in the minds of the betrayers. It was a strange thing, thought Terborg, and perhaps explained why the whites had been able to subjugate these people as they had. If all the Indian tribes had stood together against the whites, presenting a united, warlike front, the settlement of this frontier would probably have been delayed at least a score of years.

# CHAPTER TWENTY-FIVE

After the capturing, there came a time of peace for the Cheyenne. For the first time in a long, long while, there was plenty to eat, and color began to return to some of the paler faces; flesh began to return to some of the thinner ones. The snow thawed and the sky was blue, the sun bright and hot. In the warmth of mid-day, the Cheyenne women squatted outside the barracks on the bare ground, fleshing and tanning hides and rabbit skins, or they worked inside the barracks making clothing or moccasins, decorating them with beads because they had no porcupine quills to use, or sometimes just repairing the ragged clothes they had.

The men walked away from the river and along the bluffs, and occasionally came in carrying rabbits for the pot. It seemed strange to them not to be afraid, yet in all lingered a deep and hidden fear — that they would not be allowed to stay here where life could be so good but would be sent away once more as soon as the white men finished arguing about what must be done with their red-skinned wards.

Willow watched the boy and tried to tell herself that his color had improved, that his appetite was good and that new strength had come to him. All of this she knew to be untrue. He was no stronger; his color had not changed; he was as listless as before. But at least she was right about one thing. He was no worse. And she knew if he could hold his own for just a little while longer, he might begin slowly to improve.

The Cheyenne men did other things these warm fall days. They went out to sit beside the road that went from here to the Black Hills farther north. Wagons came along this road every day, and men on horseback and stagecoaches and sometimes even buggies or buckboards, carrying the white men who wanted to go to the Black Hills and look for gold.

Some of them had never seen Indians before so the coaches would stop, or the wagons stop, and the whites would get down and talk and try to trade for a beaded shirt or a pair of moccasins, offering money sometimes, or a drink from a brown bottle of whisky, or sometimes the whole bottle if the trade was good enough.

And the women would frown to see their men come home barefooted, the carefully beaded moccasins gone, but they would understand in their hearts that their men were like caged eagles now and that sometimes the white men's firewater let them forget and be wild and free again if only in their thoughts.

Or there would be horse races, weekends when the soldiers did no work and could gather and make bets on the outcome. The Cheyenne no longer had horses, so they would ride the horses of the officers, clinging like burrs to their backs, kicking them and quirting their rumps as they tried to hurry them. And everyone would yelp with excitement, eagerly laying down their bets.

Slowly and almost pleasantly, the days and weeks rolled past. The weather was mostly good, except for a few little storms that came and were quickly gone again. But no storms came with the fury of that first one in which they had been caught.

As the days passed, even though pleasantly, the uneasiness of the Cheyenne increased. The white soldier chiefs had still not said what was to be done with them and it was said in the great long barracks that they were to be sent back south except for some of their warrior men who were to be taken to Kansas and tried for the murder of the settlers there.

And the Cheyenne grew restless too. This barracks was all right for a while, until they had rested and regained their strength. But it was not right for Cheyenne to live this way. Every night they were locked in, with no privacy for anyone, not for the married couples, not for the body's necessities. The place had a smell at night like that of a village too long in one place. The Cheyenne wanted their own lodges — located upon the bank of some clear-running stream. They liked some of the soldiers and soldier chiefs but that didn't mean they wanted to live with them. Here they felt like interlopers and they wanted to feel at home.

The past weeks had been very good, but the good times were nearly over now. There was trouble in the air and the dismal certainty of death.

Two things happened almost immediately afterward, two things that brought the dismal certainty closer to reality. First, Bull Hump disappeared, and though his disappearance wasn't known for a couple of days, the time came when it could no longer be concealed. Carleton had no choice but to keep his promise to confine the Indians. If he failed to do so, he would lose them all.

So their freedom disappeared and they were confined, full time, inside the wooden barracks with even less privacy than before. Sentries walked posts outside the building, day and night. Some time later, Bull Hump returned, but it did no good. Their freedom was not restored. The gloomy certainty of the people that they were to be returned south increased.

In December, the second thing occurred. A new man arrived to relieve Colonel Carleton as Commandant. Captain Wessells was his name, and he was short-legged, light- haired, and very nervous in manner as though he was deathly afraid of this job that had been given him.

The Cheyenne lack of clothing worried Wessells, as everything else worried him. He wired Crook, who wired the Indian Bureau, which immediately wired back that warm clothing for the Cheyenne would be sent immediately. But no warm clothing came. And the time dragged by with Wessells growing more nervous all the time. At last, Crook ordered Wessells to outfit the Cheyenne from Army stores when they started south. But he did not say how to outfit children with warm clothing from Army stores. Or women either, for that matter.

At last a council was called, with Red Cloud and other Sioux offering to try and explain the situation to the increasingly sullen Cheyenne.

Wessells spoke to them first, through an interpreter. They had been ordered back to Indian Territory by the Indian Bureau and there was nothing he could do about it. He was only a soldier, following orders given to him by his superiors. He could not change the orders, he could only carry them out.

Before the Cheyenne could explode, Red Cloud rose to talk to them. He said they were foolish to think of resisting the government, which was very powerful. They had no warm clothes, no food, no horses, no weapons. There were not even white man ranches north of here from which these necessities could be stolen. Besides, there were soldiers to the north. It was best for the Cheyenne to go back south to Indian Territory. If they resisted, they would die.

Ben Terborg and Mannion, standing near the barracks door watching the council, stared at Dull Knife and the other Cheyenne chiefs. Newspapermen nearby scratched on their pads with pencils as they described the scene. At last Dull Knife arose, looking every one of his sixty-some-odd years. He told of the time when the first white men came, told of the wrongs that had been done the Indians in return for their hospitality toward those first white men. He told of the treaties made, the treaties broken by the whites, and the pencils of the newspapermen scratched almost frantically as they hurried to record his words, spoken through the interpreter.

He told of the killings, on the Sappa, the Washita, Sand Creek. And as he talked, Bull Hump rose at the back of the circle and paced back and forth like a caged wolf, his face dark as any winter sky, his eyes blazing with righteous fury, his hand never far from the handle of the knife at his belt.

"No," Dull Knife told Wessells softly but firmly all the same. "We will not go back. We are here; we are home. This is our land and we will not surrender it to you. We were promised that we could return if we did not like it in the south and we have returned. You will have to let us stay or kill us all. Our bones will bleach with the bones of the buffalo but we will not go back."

With that the council broke up, the Sioux returning to Pine Ridge, the soldier chiefs to their houses on the post. The Cheyenne stayed in the barracks, guarded even more closely now. No longer were the men permitted to go outside, even under guard, to relieve themselves but must do it inside like sick old men. The women and children were marched to the willows along the river under guard, and the guards uneasily and embarrassedly turned their backs. But they never removed their bayonets.

Gone was the camaraderie that had existed between Indian and white. Now there was only sullenness among the Indians and fear among the whites. Once more they would fight, these Indians and these whites. Once more they would kill each other because it had been decided by the Indian Bureau that they must.

Wessells waited for a while, for the holidays to pass perhaps, but he did not wait long. On the third of January, the Cheyenne were told to pack their things and move. They only shook their stubborn heads, their faces cold as stone.

But Wessells' orders were plain and he had no choice. He ordered no more food to be given to the Cheyenne. He ordered that they be given no more wood to burn in the stoves. He offered to take the women and children out, feed them and warm them in another barracks until the men gave up. But the Cheyenne sent back no answer to that.

Several days went past. The Indians did not capitulate. At last, Wessells ordered their water cut off too. They could not hold out much longer. Everyone knew that. They had to give up soon.

There had been a time, when Wessells first arrived, when he had put the Cheyenne women to work around the post. He had sent them out, under guard, to pick up papers, to shovel horse manure into wheelbarrows on the parade ground and take it away, to unload grain wagons and stores. It was healthy exercise, he said.

It *was* healthy exercise. It was also something else. It was an opportunity. Each night the Cheyenne women came in with grain or other food concealed in their blankets, to be emptied carefully into the cache beneath the barracks floor. They also brought sticks of wood, and pieces of cloth and leather, and everything else that might conceivably be of use to them.

Willow helped in this, leaving the boy she had brought north with her in the care of an old grandmother who was too weak to work. Each night she unloaded the grain she had managed to hide, usually a couple of pounds, and the few sticks of firewood she had also managed to hide. So that when the food and firewood was withdrawn from them, the Cheyenne still were not wholly without either food or wood.

The grain did not make very good food, chewed whole, or even pounded and mixed with water or even cooked afterward. But it sustained life. It kept the gnawing pains from her belly.

But when the water was withdrawn, the people began to suffer immediately from lack of it. They had nothing to mix with the dry, ground grain, and so could not eat the stuff because it only made them thirstier.

They knew they could not last. They must break out soon while they still had the strength for it. Willow heard it said that this was a plan by the soldier chiefs to get rid of them without losing any of their own. They would withhold food and water and firewood until the Cheyenne grew too weak to fight and could be killed without any risk.

Blankets were hung up over the windows so that the white sentries could not see inside and could not hear what was being said. The men sat cross-legged on the floor, that of it which had not been torn up to burn in the stoves, and their breath was visible blowing out in front of them. The women and children huddled together for warmth, the children in the center of a circle of women, some sleeping, some half-sleeping, some crying out or whimpering from hunger, or thirst, or cold.

It was decided that the men would divide themselves into two groups, to go out through the windows at opposite ends of the barracks simultaneously. The sentries would be overcome, silently if possible, and their guns and ammunition taken from them. Two of the fastest runners would go ahead to Bronson's ranch on Dead Man Creek, the closest, and secure all the horses they could but Bronson was not to be hurt.

In lowered tones, each part of the plan was carefully discussed. The moon was full; the cold as bitter as it had ever been in the memory of the old ones here, far below zero by the white man's measurement every night. But there was no help for it. They could not wait for the dark of the moon, nor could they wait for a thawing wind.

The plans were made, but by the time they were, dawn was near. So the going was put off for another night, and the men settled down uncomfortably to try and sleep out the remainder of the night.

Spotted Horse returned to Willow and the three huddled together like a family, though there was no excitement in the closeness of their bodies tonight. Their hunger and thirst were too keen, the cold too penetrating for it. Their closeness tonight was a closeness of the spirit.

When dawn came, a soldier messenger came from Wessells, ordering Wild Hog to come out and talk. Wild Hog refused, for he knew how the white men were. They would say he had agreed for the people to go south again and who could prove otherwise? So at last it was decided that he could bring someone else out with him, and Old Crow offered to go along.

A great wailing and grieving went up from the people in the icy barracks for they knew Wild Hog would not return. He would be hanged, or he would be ironed, and Old Crow with him, and they would never see him again. They needed his strength and wisdom on the trail that lay between here and the far-off Yellowstone. But, said Wild Hog, someone must go and speak for the Cheyenne. He would go.

Out he went, into the blinding glare of sun on snow, and stalked toward the little adjutant's building where the parley was to be held. Tall and gaunt, emaciated, his clothing hung from his powerful frame like rags. He went in and stood, his back to the door, facing the soldier chiefs, Captain Wessells among them scowling at him. Would the Cheyenne go south? he was asked. Would he counsel them to go south as had been ordered?

He shook his head. The answer was no. He would not promise that for the people. They must decide that for themselves and they had already decided it. They would not go south. They would rather die.

He turned to go, and the soldier guards sprang upon him, and upon Old Crow, irons in their hands. Crow was ironed easily, for he was old, but Wild Hog sprang for the door, the soldiers clinging to him the way wolves cling to an old buffalo bull, trying to bring him down. Wild Hog's hand reached his knife, and brought it out. He plunged out through the door, the soldiers still hanging from him, tearing his clothing off as he fought, but more coming until they overwhelmed him by the sheer weight of their numbers, and snapped the irons upon his wrists.

And a wailing went up in the barracks, for now they knew everything they had suspected was true. They were to be killed. And when night came again, they knew how they were to be killed — the way their relatives had been killed at Cheyenne Hole. By burning. The post blacksmith came, carrying iron chains and straps and bolts and screws. He fastened chains to the doors so that they could not be opened again.

A woman who had seen her child burned on the pyre at the Sappa began to scream. She drew her knife and sprang to kill the little ones so that they would not suffer from the burning and the smoke. Willow, who had also lost everything at the Sappa, covered her ears with her hands and bent forward and closed her eyes as tightly as she could. While Spotted Horse tried to comfort her awkwardly, she trembled, and trembled, until her teeth chattered loudly with her trembling. She could smell the smoke again, the burning flesh like roasting meat, and the smell of burning hair and hide . . . She gritted her chattering teeth to keep from screaming out. In her mind she saw Short Dog and Fat Badger once more, but the sight was blotted out by the twisted, hate-filled faces of soldiers and buffalo hunters and other whites.

Why did they hate the Indians so? Why?

The woman was disarmed, and eventually quieted, with Dull Knife scolding her in a harsh voice as though she were a child.

But her outburst had frightened others even more than the chaining of the doors had done. Weak from hunger and thirst, cold and exhausted, the Indians could not stand much more. Willow herself, though young and strong, was close to her limit of endurance, and so was Spotted Horse. He left her and joined the council of the men, and came back soon and told her, "We are going. Now. Tonight. The plan is made."

Small fires were built with the little wood that was left, these being kindled on the bare ground underneath the floorboards that had been torn up.

While some of the young men watched through tears in the blankets covering the windows to see that the guards did not slip up and fire the building, the warriors made ready to go out and fight and die. They painted their faces in the old, ceremonial way, and they put on the best clothes they had left, though even these were only rags. Feathered warbonnets came out, and the best moccasins, and rags were tied around their moccasined feet to protect them from the icy, crusted snow and bitter cold. Blankets were tied around their waists and necks, so as to leave their hands and weapons free.

Out of the hiding place beneath the floor came the five rifles hidden there, and the nine pistols, and the few cartridges and lead and powder and caps. Also the other weapons that had been hidden and saved, the knives and a few tomahawks. Carefully these things were divided, the rifles going to those who would be with the helpless ones, protecting them, a pistol each to the five Dog Soldiers who would guard the rear, delaying the soldiers and perhaps dying in doing so but giving the people time they must have to get away.

Others had weapons they had made, some with two-by-fours through which spikes from the floor had been driven until they were like ancient war clubs with spike-studded heads.

A few of the fastest runners had been chosen to carry the strongest of the children, to carry them far and fast so that the Cheyenne race would not die out but would be perpetuated forever by these strong children they had saved. Spotted Horse, because of his youth, was assigned the task of guarding the women and weaker children, and the old ones, and helping them to get away. Another young man who had been with Lame Bear when they attacked the bone wagons was also with this group, as were a few of the steadier warriors, among them the one who had led the raid on the house of Morgan Cross. He was wearing the quilted blanket he had stolen there, the one that had been hidden after Cross attacked him that first night there.

Letting the quilt be seen did not matter

now because if they got away no one would care and if they did not get away they would all be dead and beyond Cross's vengeance.

One by one the lights in the post went out. Inside the darkened barracks the Cheyenne waited, all but holding their breaths. And outside on the packed snow, the sentries paced back and forth. At a little past ten by the white man's clock, a single shot sounded from a darkened window of the darkened barracks. Outside, a guard crumpled to the snow. It is done, now, Willow thought. It is done. Whatever happens it has been decided what we must do.

# CHAPTER TWENTY-SIX

Both Morgan Cross and Orvie Watts were standing at the bar in the sutler's store when they heard the shot. For an instant both men were motionless, frozen, their breath held and listening.

Across the room two officers sat at a table and one of these was Mannion, who had come north with them. Before Mannion could make it to his feet, three more shots came close on the heels of the first, and then a crackling volley of shots, not loud, authoritative shots but weak ones, obviously from the lightly loaded guns of the Cheyenne.

No one asked what was happening. There was no need for it. All knew the Cheyenne had broken out of the log barracks, knew that they were shooting at the sentries walking their posts outside.

Cross, already running for the door, muttered savagely, "Dirty murderin' redskins!" Watts, immediately behind him, trying to get into his bulky coat as he ran, said nothing, but there was horror in his eyes.

Mannion got through the door first, and the cold was like a crackling wall outside in the snow-packed street. Cross crowded out behind him, shrugging into his coat, looking toward the barracks where the Indians were. He muttered vengefully, "They won't get far in this."

Mannion said, "Don't count on it." He was moving away even as he spoke, running toward the Indian barracks where now dim, shadowy forms were visible in the bright moonlight against the dazzling whiteness of the snow.

And out of the soldier barracks came the soldiers, almost as white as the snow in their underwear. A sargeant bawled, "Get back inside an' get your gear! You can't chase redskins in your underwear!"

Some of the men turned back, but those already outside continued to run toward the Indian barracks, firing indiscriminately as they did.

Mannion roared, "Hold your fire until you're sure what you're shooting at! The sentries are down there and there are women and children . . ." His voice trailed off, as though he had suddenly realized how useless that warning was. You can't tell a blanket-wrapped squaw from a blanket-wrapped buck at night and besides there wasn't one in twenty soldiers that even cared. An Indian was an Indian.

Cross ran after Mannion, his revolver in his hand. This was the time he had waited so patiently for here at Fort Robinson. This was what he had stayed to see. They were there, ahead of him, the Indians who had raided his ranch, burned his house and killed his family. Tonight he would avenge that raid. Tonight he would take a life for each member of his family, four lives in all, including the one he had seen wearing Nellie's quilt.

But now the Indians were shooting at them. Mannion ducked behind the building and Cross dived in beside him as a bullet tore up a shower of snow immediately in front of him. Watts came plunging in behind the building too.

Indians were pouring from the windows, while others knelt in the snow and fired at the oncoming, underwear-clad troops. Beside each window were two men, helping those inside out into the snow. As they dropped to the ground, the Cheyenne hurried away, carrying bundles, most of them, or blanket-wrapped children or infants, or a little bit of food or firewood. Down toward the river they ran, almost ghostly as they lost themselves in the willows. But there was nothing ghostly about the dark forms that lay silent and still on the hard-packed snow.

Nothing ghostly about these, three sentries, and at least as many Indians.

Breathing hard, Cross broke from behind the corner and charged toward the barracks again, firing now as he ran. Mannion roared, "Cross! Damn you, put that gun away! You're a civilian and . . ." Again he stopped, as though realizing he was wasting breath. Watts burst from the corner and ran after Cross, also holding a gun in his hand. Mannion followed the two of them, running hard.

A bugle sounded now, its notes clear and far-carrying in the still, frigid air, echoing back from the bluffs behind the post. Fully-dressed soldiers, some still shrugging into their heavy coats, now ran from the barracks toward the stables. Some of those clad in underwear turned and ran back toward their barracks, violently shivering, their teeth chattering audibly.

Cross stopped, steadied his gun and fired at one of the shadowy Indian forms coming out of the window fifty feet away. He missed, hearing his bullet strike a metal window hinge and go ricocheting away into space, humming like a bee. He fired again, then dropped when one of the Indians opened up on him.

Watts flung himself down on top of

Cross. He jammed the gun into Cross's side. "Drop your gun, Cross, or I'll blow a hole in you!"

"What the hell? You gone crazy or somethin'?"

"Drop it! One of them bucks might be my kid."

Mannion reached the pair. He halted and stood there briefly. A rifle flashed over near the Indian barracks and Mannion whirled around, grunted and sat down. He said numbly, "I'm hit."

Cross got to his knees, ignoring Watts now, and shoved his revolver into the holster at his side. He put an arm around Mannion and got to his feet, lifting Mannion as he did. He turned and the two staggered away toward the post hospital.

Watts remained where he was. Indians were still coming from the barracks windows, the older ones now, the weak and crippled ones. An oldster fell from one of the windows and crumpled to the snow. Watts could hear his moan of pain. The old Indian tried to get up, but could not because one leg would not support his weight. It was twisted at an odd angle and Watts knew instantly that it was broken.

The old man crawled away at right angles to the direction all the others were going.

He made it to a bank of shoveled snow and lay there helplessly, unable to get over it. Watts heard his voice, old and cracked and quavering, singing a Cheyenne death song as he waited for death to come.

He did not wait long. All the people were out of the barracks now, the last of them straggling away toward the river. Only the dead ones were left, and the old man with the broken leg.

Underwear-clad troopers charged in beneath the barracks windows, some with bayonets fixed to their rifles. One ran to the old man, put the gun muzzle against his head. Even then, Watts did not realize the man meant to shoot. But the muzzle flash came and the old man's brains and blood splattered out, making a dark spot against the banked-up snow.

Down at the edge of the willows Dog Soldiers in the Cheyenne rear guard opened up on the troopers from behind a high bank of drifted snow. The soldiers sought cover momentarily but then, rallied by their officers, charged ahead, massing as they did. Few of them still wore no clothes. Most of those who had come out in their underwear had gone back by now. There were even a few with horses, ready to give chase through the willows, across the river and up into the sheltering bluffs beyond.

Orvie realized he was praying sound-lessly. "Oh God, let 'em get away!" He seemed to be one with the Cheyenne to-night, as though he had never left their vil-lages, as though the past twenty years had been suddenly and miraculously erased.

But the Dog Soldiers did not get away. The sounds of their revolvers died and the soldiers charged the drift, plowing through it, firing again and again into the bodies of the Dog Soldiers who had died so bravely. Five lay there in the drift and back at the barracks lay the old man and three others, all with from half a dozen to a dozen wounds in them. Only one had been wounded and lived, Tangle Hair, who had dragged himself off to one side and called to some soldiers in pidgin Sioux and been rec-ognized.

Orvie Watts got to his feet and walked over to the old one who lay in his own blood, part of his skull carried away by the soldier's bullet fired from so very close. He stared down at the old man's gaunt, lined face looking up at the mercilessly bright moon and suddenly he began to shake. He turned away and walked to where the five Dog Sol-diers lay. Already their guns had been seized for souvenirs, and their headdresses and even, from two of them, their moccasins. Orvie began to curse, softly and almost soundlessly, but with an awful bitterness. One of these could have been his son. He went from one to the other, kneeling each time to look into a face. But all were older than his son. All were tough, experienced warriors, the best the Cheyenne had.

He was ashamed of his own relief as he got up. He returned toward the barracks, hearing the shouting and shooting and crashing there in the willows and beyond, the calling back and forth of the disorganized troopers, and the bawled orders of their officers and non-commissioned officers. He stopped at each Indian body, kneeling and looking at the face.

He remembered the stand of buffalo down near the Smoky Hill River so long ago. He remembered the bite of powder-smoke in his nose, and the smell of blood and death, and the sound, the roaring of his Sharps, the terrified bawling of the uneasy buffalo.

Almost dazedly he walked, the confusion growing around him, the sounds of the chase fading out there in the river bottoms, then swelling in a burst of fire southwest where the sawmill was. Suddenly he found himself in front of the post hospital and he was crowded inside by troopers helping the wounded along, and carrying those who were too badly hurt to walk. Inside the door he stepped aside and stood there staring. He saw Mannion sitting on a bench with blood turning the shoulder of his tunic red. Mannion's face was gray with pain, but his eyes met Orvie's briefly and Orvie crossed the room to him. He said, "I'm sorry, Lieutenant. I'm sorry it had to be you."

Mannion smiled faintly. "At least I don't have to be out there killing them."

Watts didn't reply. He was looking around for Cross. Mannion said, "He brought me here and left. He'll kill his share before he stops."

Watts nodded. He put a hand on Mannion's unhurt one and gripped it briefly. "Good luck, Lieutenant."

Mannion nodded, faintly smiling still. Watts turned and hurried out. Once outside he ran toward the stable.

Passing through officer country on his way, he heard Congressman Terborg's roaring voice. "God damn you, Wessells, get out there and control your men! Or do you mean to let them get rid of your problem for you before you take command?"

He did not hear Wessells' reply, but ran

on, the sub-zero air biting the inside of his nose as he breathed.

There was little he could do, he realized. The Indians were largely beyond his help.

Yet he knew one thing. Cross had to be stopped.

None of the Cheyenne inside the barracks, while planning this, had believed it could be this bad. No one had thought the soldiers could get out of their barracks so fast.

It was like it had been all the other places where Cheyenne had been slaughtered, the soldiers out of the control of their officers, firing blindly and recklessly at everything that moved. Two women and several children were killed along the river, and shot again by soldiers coming along behind, and shot again, and again. After that they were stripped of moccasins, and ornaments, and knives until there was nothing left to take, nothing worthwhile for souvenirs.

Willow ran swiftly after she dropped from the window, after she turned and caught the boy as he dropped into her arms. She ran after the others like a deer, the snow squeaking beneath her feet, the guns roaring back there almost as soon as she disappeared into the willows that lined the river bank.

At the river, lined on both sides with ice but flowing swift and deep in the center, people flung themselves down flat, the burning thirst of days tormenting them, needing a drink now if they died for it. Willow also flung herself down, but she let the boy drink first, gulping and choking and gulping again as though he could never get enough. She drank then, but only enough to kill the searing thirst, and then was up again.

Hundreds of soldiers were coming on behind, with a great noise of shooting and yelling, and there seemed to be no effort now to control them any more. Willow glanced back once, hesitated, then, holding the boy high plunged into the icy stream and across, getting soaked almost to the waist.

Out again on the other side, with her clothing freezing and sticking to the ice so that it had to be torn loose by sheer force. Behind her came Spotted Horse, helping an old woman, almost carrying her, but hurrying to keep up with Willow and the boy.

Willow's clothes were like iron now, but she had no time to think of that. On she ran, up the snow-drifted slope toward the bluffs, toward the place where they might, for an instant, rest and be safe.

Behind the killing went on, as the weaker ones slowed or dropped from weakness or exhaustion. A few prisoners were taken, most of them wounded, some very seriously. In the first half mile, half the men were killed, the others scattering, helping where they could, making a stand to protect the flight of others when they must. And over it all the moon shone pitilessly down, revealing each moccasin track in the flawless snow, showing each dark figure as it climbed the drifted slope toward the protection of the bluffs.

Small groups formed from scattered individuals. With Willow was Spotted Horse and the old woman whose name was Cut Nose, and after a while they were joined by Lame Bear and another man who had been shot in the thigh and who left a bright red trail of blood behind.

Halfway up the slope they were joined by another man, who was helping along an older man and a young boy, and a woman in middle age.

On and on they went, knowing they were leaving a plain wide trail but unable to do differently. And below them, Cheyenne were pursued and killed, like mice flushed from a haystack and pursued as they scattered by the cat.

★ ★ ★

Halfway up the bluff they had to stop. They could go no farther — not without rest, not without a chance to warm themselves. Their limbs moved like mechanical things; their clothes, soaked at the river crossing, were like iron casings over their lower bodies. Their hands and feet were numb, the hands too numb to hold a clump of brush or draw back a hammer on a gun or pull the trigger afterward. And some of them had wounds.

At first there was nothing any of them could do but clear a little place in the snow and huddle down, so that they could warm each other just by being close. The wounded ones were inside, the children and women next, the men on the outside of the little group, one side against the bitter cold, but with their arms and hands in where they could be warmed and thus made workable again. The fighting was not over yet, nor the dying, and their hands and weapons would be needed soon.

Willow was crowded tight against Spotted Horse on the one side and the boy on the other. All the way she had carried the boy close against her, blanket-wrapped, to protect him from the cold. She knew how faint was the spark of life in him, how easily it could be extinguished, particularly now that there was neither food nor warmth for him.

For a while it was good just to rest, and let her breathing become slow and regular again. It was good to feel warmth creeping back into her arms and legs and feet, even though the returning blood brought pain so great she moaned softly and could not seem to stop.

Others were moaning too, but softly, from the pain of wounds and from frozen hands or feet.

Down below, in the direction of the post, Willow saw four cavalrymen spurring their plunging horses through the deep drifts up the slope in pursuit. Great clouds of frozen breath streamed ahead from the horses' nostrils. The men rode balanced in the stirrups against the unsteady plunging motion of their mounts. They had found the trail and even though they had not yet identified this dark place here, they soon would, and would then begin firing.

Lame Bear's voice was fierce, like the warning snarl of the wolf. "You must go now, while we hold them back."

Willow started up the slope again, toward a towering face of sandstone bluff gleaming white in the bright moonlight, carrying the boy and helping Cut Nose who seemed very weak, perhaps from a wound she had not said anything about. Behind her came the middle-aged woman, who was Blue Bird, helping the boy who was even younger than Spotted Horse, perhaps no more than ten.

Lame Bear, and Spotted Horse, and the man who had been shot in the thigh and who had bled heavily upon the snow — these three stayed behind along with the oldster who had been with Bluebird and the boy. Between the four they had two guns, one an old muzzle-loading rifle and one a revolving percussion pistol in which only two loads remained. And they had a single knife.

Fifty feet above, Willow stopped, and looked longingly back, knowing she would never see Spotted Horse again. He was gone, as Short Dog was gone, as Fat Badger was also gone. She had obtained another family but she had not been allowed to keep it very long. But she still had the boy, and she promised herself she would not lose him too. She turned and pressed on, softly urging those with her to keep up else they would be killed when Lame Bear and the others were overrun down below. They must make use of the sacrifice of the men by getting away. Otherwise the lives of those brave men would be wasted and of no use.

They were almost to the foot of the great sandstone face when the soldiers began firing.

It was easy to tell their guns from those of the Cheyenne. Their reports were loud, echoing back from the rock faces up above, and filling the ears with sound. By contrast, the reports of Cheyenne guns were weak, but their bullets could kill just as surely as those of the soldiers, if the range was close enough.

"Maybe the heathens are dead!" yelled one of the cavalrymen. "Looks like we're goin' to get ourselves some souvenirs!"

Another shouted warningly, "Watch out! They might be playing possum!"

Before his words died out, Lame Bear fired the old muzzle-loading ride, its smoke billowing out black in the bright moonlight. And suddenly one of the cavalry horses' saddles was empty and there was a dark spot on the snow that did not move.

The others tried to whirl their horses and retreat down the heavily drifted slope, but the bark of the revolver came, and another saddle was empty there.

The two remaining now turned their horses and held them still, while they poured a withering fire into the huddled Indians. Lame Bear fired the last remaining pistol load, and one of the horses, hit, turned and began to buck away down the slope. A hundred yards down, he fell, raising a monstrous cloud of snow, rolling and throwing his rider clear. The man got up and, covered with snow, hurriedly limped down the slope.

The last man whirled his horse and retreated until he was out of range. There he stopped and stared up at the little group of Indians uncertainly.

Lame Bear stood up for a moment. Then he knelt, to look at the man who had been wounded in the thigh. The man was dead, his life a stain underneath his leg, spreading scarlet in the snow. The oldster was also hit, in the chest, and every time he moved he coughed uncontrollably. "Go and save yourselves," he choked. "I cannot go farther."

Lame Bear hesitated. The old one said, "Save the women and this boy. Our people must not all die."

Lame Bear turned to Spotted Horse. "Go!" His voice was sharp and harsh. He watched Spotted Horse run up the slope, carrying the empty rifle which could be reloaded later. He thrust the empty pistol into his belt, then plunged down to the nearest cavalryman. He seized the man's carbine and ammunition pouch, turned and climbed after Spotted Horse. Farther down the slope, the last of the four cavalrymen fired at him methodically, his bullets kicking up little puffs of snow wherever they struck. But none of them hit Lame Bear and he went on until he reached the others, halted at the very foot of the sandstone bluff.

Here, there was a little dry and rocky ground, that would not easily hold a trail unless a trail of blood was left upon the rocks. Here, too, there was a little shadow, hiding them from eyes searching down below. Others would come after them, but by then perhaps they would be far away from here.

Bleakly the five adults and the two children stared at the moon-washed valley below, at the winking lanterns in some of the soldiers' hands. Even at this distance they could hear the confusion of shouts, of creaking wagon wheels and double-trees, of plunging horses' hoofs and slamming doors and bugling. A death wagon began going around to gather up frozen bodies, most of them already stripped of everything that was valuable as souvenirs. But still there was no order among the troops, several hundred of them scattered out the length and breadth of the valley here, searching out a few hidden Indians and killing them or sometimes making prisoners of them.

Lame Bear said, "Come," and led away, choosing now the path that would leave the least trail across this rocky ground from which the snow had thawed. Horses could come this far, but he knew there were paths by which he and those with him could get up through the bluffs, where horses could not follow them. There, they would have a little respite from the hunt, for the soldiers riding horses would have to go up the valley six or seven miles to the nearest place where they could climb out on top.

They followed him dumbly, glad for his protection and counsel, glad to place their trust in him. And Spotted Horse brought up the rear. He had grown to manhood very fast this night. Willow looked back at him and made a little weary smile.

# CHAPTER TWENTY-SEVEN

Morgan Cross charged out of the post hospital, stood for a moment glancing up and down, then ran in the direction of the stable. He had no rifle, but he had the revolver he always carried in a holster at his side and the loops of his cartridge belt were full. Besides that he had a burning thirst — to avenge Nellie and Jess and his two silken-haired little girls.

Halfway to the stable he stopped. There was the racket of firing everywhere, but suddenly, straight ahead of him on the snowy slope, he saw four horses and beyond a dark spot that had to be a group of huddled Indians. As he watched, shots blossomed up there, the sounds echoing back from the towering sandstone bluff.

One of the saddles emptied, and suddenly another, and then a horse came catapulting down the slope, raising an enormous cloud of powdered snow. The horse lay still but the man, thrown clear, got to his feet and came limping down toward Cross, covered with snow and white from head to foot.

Cross saw the other cavalryman sit his

horse up on the slope, firing methodically at the huddled group of Indians. But they went on, or some of them did, and at last the cavalryman came sliding his horse on his haunches down the slope. He rode past Cross without speaking, heading for the post hospital, perhaps to get help for his fallen comrades.

He wouldn't need a horse, thought Cross. There, on the slope above him were Indians, Cheyenne Indians, perhaps even the one who had worn his wife's quilt that first night here. Or if not, then others of equal guilt. The four who had attacked his place were not the only ones who had killed.

Without further thought, he began his ascent. The slope was steep and drifted deep with snow. In places he sank almost to his waist but he continued to fight upward stubbornly. He reached the dead horse and rested a moment and then went on. The Indians had all disappeared now. Ahead there were two black spots in the snow where two had died.

Cross was aware that he might be climbing to his death. But he didn't care. Life held nothing for him now, nothing but memories, of a petal-soft cheek laid trustingly against his, of the tickle of a wisp of silk-fine hair against a nostril, of a sturdy, blue-eyed look of self dependence from a growing son, the sort of look that makes a man's heart proud.

He reached the two Indians lying in the snow. In the bright moonlight he could see the bloodstained snow beneath one of them. The other . . .

Suddenly that one moved. Making a sound like a lung-shot deer, the man threw himself at Cross, moonlight glinting bright on the shining blade of the knife he held in his hand.

It cut through pants and boot leather and deep into Morgan Cross's leg. Coughing, but coughing with a strange choked sound, the man fell back. Morgan snatched his revolver and fired twice, but the man was already dead. An oldster, who must have been twice Morgan's age, he had been dead before the bullets struck.

Nausea came over Morgan Cross. He sat down in the snow, staring dumbly at his leg, now streaming blood. He stared at the old man, whose face was upturned toward the moon.

Gaunt and emaciated, strong and patient and calm, it reminded him suddenly and unaccountably of his father's face. He felt his head begin to whirl, and heard a shout downslope toward the noisy post in the valley below. Looking that way, he saw another man climbing up toward him.

Long before the man reached him, he knew it was Orvie Watts. Watts halted once to rest briefly and then came on. He stopped where Morgan was and sank down into the snow. He glanced at the two dead Indians and then at Cross's leg. He said, "Well, you've got two of them, looks like."

"I didn't get 'em. But one of them got me. You got anything you could tie around my goddam leg?"

Orvie took off his coat, then removed his shirt. He put the coat back on, buttoned it, then knelt, bringing out his knife. He slit Cross's pants up to the knee, then slit the boot-top down so that he could get at the wound. He tore the shirt and began to bind the strips around the wound. "Steady bleeding, Cross. It didn't get no artery."

Cross waited, motionless, until he had finished, his breathing slow and deep, the nausea coming and going in waves. Orvie said, "I'll help you back down the hill to the post hospital."

"To hell with that. I'm going on."

"To kill your Indians? Haven't enough of them died tonight?"

"Not for me." He felt compelled to explain, but he couldn't explain. There was too much to it to explain to another man. All he knew was that he had to go on. He had to kill, once for Nellie, once for Jess, once each for the two little girls if he was ever going to live at peace with himself again.

Watts was staring strangely at him. He said, "You're crazy. Hell, you're crazy as a damn hoot owl."

Cross stared coldly at him. "I guess you ought to know. You killed a couple of 'em once yourself. For less reason too." He was instantly sorry for what he'd said, but he couldn't take the words back now. And a strange, angry stubbornness prevented him from saying he was sorry for what he'd said.

Watts didn't reply. He just stared out across the moon-washed valley of death, his face twisted. Cross got up sullenly and began to climb toward the foot of the great rock face above. Watts silently followed him.

Climbing now, Morgan Cross could see no Indians up above against the face of rock. But he knew that they were there. This was no hunt for helpless game, like the buffalo or deer, that ran but did not fight back. The Cheyenne had weapons and were dangerous, the men, the women, even the children and the old ones, like that old man back there who had slashed him with a knife. No one could say he was hunting helpless people for his revenge. He was risking his own life going after them. And he was wounded too.

Behind him Orvie Watts climbed patiently, puffing hard from exertion, sometimes slipping and falling in the snow, but coming on. Watts had fathered one of these Indians twenty years ago. Cross had heard that from somebody. And Watts was looking for his son.

Suddenly this seemed very strange to him. Watts was probably following him to try and prevent him from killing Indians, particularly any twenty-year-old males. So he had Indians in front of him and an Indian lover behind. He grunted with pain each time he put his foot down, each time he put his weight on the wounded leg. His eyes watered from the cold and his nose kept dripping, the droplet sometimes freezing on the end of it. The insides of his nostrils drew together, freezing briefly with each indrawn breath, thawing again each time that he exhaled. And the pain began down in the knife-slashed leg. The cold made it throb and burn excruciatingly.

He reached the foot of the sandstone rim and paused, leaning against the rock while he caught his breath. He stared down into the valley at the lights moving about like fireflies. Occasionally a shot boomed out, echoing from the bluffs behind the post, but sounding harmless at this distance.

Breathing normally again, Cross looked to left and right, trying to decide which way the Indians had gone. He listened intently for some sound, but heard none and at last fumbled beneath his coat and brought out a match. Cupping it against the slight breeze up here, he knelt and struck it against the rock.

It flickered feebly, inches from the ground. Moving along, it caught the bright red of a drop of blood in its light and farther on, two more and still farther, another one. Returning, Cross found a little pool of blood where Watts was standing and where the wounded Indian must have stood. It had already frozen solid there on the rocks. He said, "That way," indicating the direction with a toss of his head.

Watts touched his sleeve. "Why the hell don't you wait? The government'll find out which of 'em killed your family. They'll be tried an' hanged for what they did. Chances are these Indians we're followin' didn't have nothin' to do with it."

"Did the government do anything about

that quilt I found? You're damn right they didn't! They just gave me hell for jumpin' the buck that was wearin' it."

Watts did not reply, so Cross went on, edging along the foot of the bluff over bare rocks here where the sun had melted all the snow. He went slowly and as quietly as he could, knowing how good Cheyenne were at laying ambushes. Watts followed silently.

They traveled cautiously for nearly a quarter mile before they came to a break in the rim, where a rocky way led up . . . Again Cross struck a match, kneeling and studying the rocks. He nodded as he threw the match down. "They went up here."

Snow had drifted heavily in places, and wherever there was snow the blood could be seen, the droplets that showed up darkly against the snow, and sometimes a clotted mass so that Cross knew whoever had the wound was gut-shot and bleeding heavily. He had trailed deer once or twice that were gut-shot and he knew how far they could travel with such a wound. Yet he could also imagine the pain a person felt, and in this cold . . .

He scowled, angry and irritated at himself. He forced himself to think of Nellie and when thought of her did not feed the outrage within him, he thought of Jess and the two little girls, burning in the pyre of their home, perhaps not even dead but burned alive . . .

Above, where moonlight bathed the upper end of this slash through the rim, he suddenly saw dark shapes against the snow. He snapped his gun up level and fired twice. The dark shapes abruptly disappeared.

Almost running now, he scrambled upward over the rocks, halting at the top when a gun flared almost in his face. He raised his own gun again, thumbing the hammer back, only to feel himself struck from behind, struck by Orvie Watts's body flung hard against his legs.

He toppled back, his gun discharging from reflex at the sky. Furious, he fought his way to his feet, swinging the gun flat at Orvie as he rose.

It struck Orvie's head and the man crumpled without a sound. Cross lunged on through the deep drifted snow up a steep pitch to the level plain. He stared at the black shapes hurrying across the dazzling expanse of snow. He turned his head and looked behind uncertainly.

With a curse he jammed the revolver into its holster, swung around and went back to where Orvie lay.

Watts was stirring. He sat up, putting a

mittened hand to his head. He stared at Cross, silently accusing him.

Cross glared down at him. His breath came in short, shallow gasps and his eyes blazed furiously. He said between his teeth, "God damn you, if you do that again, I'll knock your head in for you."

Orvie got slowly to his feet, holding his head slightly cocked against the pain in it. He said, "Forget it, Cross. Let 'em go."

Cross heard voices down below. He stared past Orvie, down the steep trail to the rimrock base. Two troopers were toiling up. Cross yelled, "Up here! There's five or six Indians ahead of us!"

Orvie Watts released a long, slow sigh. The two troopers reached them and the four climbed to the level of the plain and set out grimly in pursuit of the Indians, trailing without difficulty through the snow.

Spotted Horse was stumbling as he ran to catch up with Willow and the boy. Twice his leg gave out beneath him and he fell, only to rise again and hurry on. Reaching the others, he turned his head and glanced behind. He could not see the white man any more. The man must have turned and gone back to the other one.

Willow said worriedly, "You're hurt!"

He nodded. "In the leg," and added when she would have put the boy down and examined it, "Not now. It will be all right until we have put more distance between ourselves and them."

Willow hurried on, holding the boy close against her breast. Both her feet were numb now, and one of her hands. Her face felt stiff and sore. The boy was very quiet, but she could feel his breath, warm against her cheek.

A quarter mile from the rim, Cut Nose finally sank into the snow, her hand held firmly against her side. Willow knelt without putting down the boy. Cut Nose said weakly, "I cannot go on. Leave me and save yourselves."

Lame Bear came back and knelt by Cut Nose too. "Where are you hit?"

"Here." The old woman brought her hand away from her wound. It was dark with blood. Lame Bear looked at Willow. He nodded and Willow got to her feet. She was thinking that if there had only been a few clouds tonight to hide the moon, Cut Nose and Spotted Horse would not have been wounded. Others would not have died. The men sent to Bronson's ranch would have gotten horses and brought them back and the people would have escaped as it had been planned. But there had been no clouds, and most of the people were dead. By morning perhaps all would be dead.

No one slept at Fort Robinson that night. The surgeon and his assistants worked tirelessly as the beds in the post hospital filled up with frozen, bleeding, ragged and half-starved Indians. There was a boy of no more than five with a bullet-shattered elbow, the lower arm drenched with blood and with tiny fragments of bone the blood had washed out of the wound. He was conscious but he made no sound, only staring with terror at the white people moving about from place to place. There was a young woman, wounded in the breast by the same bullet that had smashed her infant's head, clutching the dead infant close to her, refusing to look down at it, refusing to admit that it was dead. She fought like a wildcat when they tried to take the child from her, so the surgeon gave her a massive shot of morphine and then waited for it to take effect before trying to take the child again. More than once the eyes of this man filmed over, and more than once his throat threatened to close up. More than once he muttered an almost soundless and bitterly savage curse to himself, and then went on, working tirelessly.

# CHAPTER TWENTY-EIGHT

Up on the plain above the canyon of White River the trail of the Indians pointed north, ever north toward Hat Creek which would afford the next concealment from those pursuing them.

But Morgan Cross was close now, pushing hard because he knew how elusive they could be. Just behind him came Orvie Watts, his eyes narrowed against the excruciating pain in his head, wincing sometimes when a certain movement made it throb unbearably. Behind Watts were the two troopers, carbines ready in their hands.

The moon slid toward the western horizon but the trail led on across the unblemished whiteness of the drifted snow. The sky in the east turned gray and the gray spread across the sky, but still the trail led on.

The ambush was carefully planned. It was laid at a spot where the land fell away so that Cross and Watts and the two with them could not see that the trail did not continue beyond this place.

Here, at the crest of this little rise, the snow had drifted deep, making enough depth so that the Indians could burrow into it, covering themselves, hiding like mice in a pile of loose, dry hay. Blue Bird and the ten-year-old boy and Willow and her boy went on beyond the men, if Spotted Horse could be called a man. And when the ambush had been made, Lame Bear slashed Spotted Horse's trouser leg to expose the bullet wound so that he could look at it.

It was a nasty tear and the blood pumped steadily from it, coming in regular, bright-red spurts. Lame Bear said nothing, nor did Willow, who knew what the regular pumping meant. But her eyes rested softly on the youth's pale face. Her icy hand went out and touched his hand.

Lame Bear packed snow around the wound, then tied a rag over it to hold the snow in place. He had seen that done by a medicine man once, and had heard that the cold helped slow the flow of blood. But Willow stared at the young man's face, seeing the grayness of death in his skin, the dullness of it in his eyes. He had lost too much blood and he would die. They would all die, she thought. There was no longer any hope.

Lame Bear finished with the boy's leg and turned again to watch the plain lying toward the south. Willow carefully raised her own head and saw the four specks toiling toward them across the frozen waste, less than half a mile away.

Lame Bear loaded the carbine taken from the cavalryman back beneath the bluff and laid a handful of cartridges nearby. He loaded the other rifle, the muzzle loader, though this took longer because his hands were numb and half frozen and did not work very well. Then he began the task of loading the revolver. He only got three chambers loaded before Willow whispered to him, "They are very close, Lame Bear."

He raised his head cautiously and saw that they were indeed very close. He roused Spotted Horse, who had drowsed off. He pushed the muzzle-loading rifle into the boy's hands. "Do not fire until they are almost upon us. You must get one of them with the one ball in this gun. There will be no time to reload."

Spotted Horse fought to rouse himself, succeeding partially. Lame Bear gave the revolver to Willow. "There are but three shots. You must not shoot until you are very sure."

She nodded, taking the gun in her stiff, numb hand and holding it against her body to warm it and her hand.

Lame Bear scooped up several handfuls

of snow and covered his head with it. Cautiously, he raised up to look.

Almost instantly he poked the rifle ahead of him, pulled back the hammer, sighted carefully and fired. And now, Willow also raised her head, as did Spotted Horse.

Lame Bear's first shot had missed cleanly, perhaps because he had never fired such a carbine before. He reloaded as quickly as he could with his stiff, half frozen fingers, sighted and fired again.

His target was smaller this time than it had been before because all four white men had flung themselves prone in the snow, but his success was better anyway. One of the cavalrymen began to howl, raising up and clawing at his rump. Lame Bear reloaded and shot again and this time the cavalryman was slammed back and knocked prone. He laid completely still.

The white men were arguing. The one Lame Bear had stolen the mules from back in Kansas, recognizable by his voice which Lame Bear knew anyway, shouted, "Cross, give 'em a chance to give up!"

But no demand for surrender came. Only bullets came, tearing into the snow and sending little showers of it over the crouching Indians. Again the voice yelled, "Cross!"

One of the men got up, not the one who had yelled or the trooper, but the man with yellow hair and wild blue eyes. He charged toward the Indians, his revolver ready in his hand. Slipping and staggering in the deep, treacherous snow, he came on, pursued by the bone picker, Orvie Watts and by the remaining trooper, his young eyes wide and scared.

Lame Bear fired, and heard the bullet strike the trooper, heard it like the swiftest of echoes. Almost frantically he grabbed for another cartridge from the little pile.

Perhaps he was too anxious; perhaps he tried to be too swift. But his fingers did not close on another cartridge. Instead his hand scattered the pile, scattered the cartridges in the snow.

Taking his eyes off the men charging toward him, he yelled, "Spotted Horse!" and clawed frantically for a cartridge with which to reload his gun. Spotted Horse reared up, raising the old rifle to his shoulder, his eyes burning now, his face momentarily flushed. He fired the muzzle loader and a cloud of smoke billowed out obscuring the white men momentarily.

There was time for nothing else. Cross and the trooper came over the little ridge, looming up there, dark against the gray sky and dazzling whiteness of snow. The mortally wounded trooper fired, and the woman, Blue Bird, gave a sharp little sound of shock. Cross fired and Lame Bear slammed back against Willow, knocking her prone, covering her with his body, half-burying her.

Her mouth was full of snow, her face buried in it, she did not release the gun. All she could think of now was the boy, who had been crouched at her side, silent and big eyed and still.

She heard the bone picker screech, "Cross! You got Lame Bear an' he's the only one that knew . . . !" There was a violent scuffling in the rifle pit and then two revolver shots, loud and deafening and practically in her ears, and after that there was nothing. No sound at all.

She fought her way clear of Lame Bear's body and glanced fearfully at the other bodies lying scattered here. Lame Bear was dead, his throat half torn away by a bullet. He had soaked one of her legs with the blood, which had poured out of him in a torrent, gone in seconds, stopped when his heart stopped pumping it. Spotted Horse was also dead, though she saw no new wound. Blue Bird was dead, the boy she held against her breast killed by the same bullet that had killed her. Willow was the only one left, and the boy she had carried north with her, now trembling violently with fear, his eyes filled with tears, his teeth chattering but making no other sound.

And the white men . . . Cross was down. His body was sprawled across that of Spotted Horse but his chest still rose and fell. Orvie Watts was also down, but Orvie Watts was dead. His eyes were open, staring at the sky, and there was a bluish hole in his forehead from which a small trickle of bright blood oozed. The trooper was also dead, wounded by Lame Bear and finished by Spotted Horse's single shot.

Numbly Willow stared. There was no life here save for her life, that of the boy, and the life of Morgan Cross, the one with yellow hair who had lost his family down near Cheyenne Hole.

Numbly she stared down at him, the revolver in her hand. She must kill him, she said to herself over and over but there had already been too much killing here. Besides, it didn't seem to matter any more.

But if she did not kill him, then she had better go. She stooped, gathering up the things that would help keep her alive; things that were no longer needed here by these dead. She took the carbine Lame Bear had taken from the dead trooper back beneath the bluff, and the cartridges for it, which she found by digging around in the snow. She took Lame Bear's blanket and tore it into strips which she wound around her feet and around those of the boy, who just sat in the snow and looked at her. She took Blue Bird's blanket for the boy and Spotted Horse's blanket for herself.

She wished she had some food but she did not. That would have to come later. Perhaps she would find a cow, or a deer, or a horse. Or she might find others who had also escaped death last night.

She picked up the boy and started away, falling almost immediately because of the depth of the snow. She got up and struggled on, looking back once at the dead lying where this little stand had been made.

She was alone again now, more alone than ever before in her life. She had lost her first family at Sand Creek, and now she had lost everything except this boy. She did not know how she was going to keep him alive in this icy, frozen waste, for he needed food, and warmth, and the ministering of a medicine man to bring him back to health and life.

Moving almost deliberately, she toiled away, heading again toward the north country on the Yellowstone. She might die, of hunger, of cold, of exhaustion or hopelessness, but she would never go back now. She would never turn her face away from this promised homeland in the north.

Morgan Cross was numb when he regained consciousness. He thought he had never been so cold in his entire life. He put up a hand to his head. The blood which had welled from the wound above his ear had frozen there, except for a small spot immediately over the wound, which still seeped blood.

He struggled to his feet, wincing with pain in his wounded leg, with pain that pounded through his head, with pain in his nearly frozen hands. The revolver he had been holding fell from his nerveless fingers and was lost in the snow. He stared around him unbelievingly.

Four dead Indians were here, the middle-aged buck, the squaw, and the two young boys. He wondered if they were a family. A family like his own.

Strangely enough, there seemed to be no hate in him any more. There was nothing. All he wanted now was to leave this place, to go home, to forget. He didn't know for sure how many of these Indians he had killed himself. He did know he had killed the bone picker, Orvie Watts. In self-defense, perhaps, but he had killed the man all the same. Because Watts had tried to prevent him from killing the buck, Lame Bear.

He stood there covered with snow and hunched against the cold, staring around at the endless frozen land. And suddenly his eyes caught the trail Willow had made, going north.

He stared along it for a long, long time, then numbly turned his head and stared back toward Fort Robinson. Then, knowing he had to see this through to the end he took the trail and struggled northward almost like some kind of machine, leaving a trail of his own blood in the snow. He didn't know that this lone survivor was a woman. Things had been happening too fast back there to identify anyone, even by sex or age. Suddenly he saw the black speck ahead of him, toiling laboriously through the snow. Perhaps half a mile was between them. Cross forced himself to go faster, and slowly began to reduce the distance separating them.

The gray of the day did not change as the sun rose into the sky. The cloud cover was too thick even for the sun's light to penetrate. After a while the wind stiffened and began to drift the snow, blowing it in great, high, blinding clouds.

For long periods, the figure ahead of Cross was hidden from his sight. But the trail remained, though there was some danger that it would drift over and be forever lost to him.

Exertion had warmed him, and strengthened him. His head still throbbed and his leg still pained, but both were bearable. And a new urgency now came over him. Catching this lone Indian seemed more important than anything he had ever done before.

Slowly, slowly, he closed the distance separating them, to a quarter mile, to three hundred yards, to two hundred, to a hundred yards. Fifty yards back from Willow and the boy, he perceived that there were two, and that she was a woman, carrying a child.

And at almost the same instant she stopped, crouched down in the blinding drifting snow, and leveled her rifle at him.

Cross instantly dropped prone. Her shot rolled out, its sound all but lost in the wind and whipping clouds of snow.

Instantly Cross was on his feet, lunging ahead, pumping frantically with his legs, trying to reach her before she could reload. He could see her working frantically, her frozen fingers all but refusing to work at all. She got the rifle's action open and fumbled for a shell. While he was still fifteen feet away, she managed to drop the shell into the chamber and slam the breech. The gun came up, its muzzle and barrel black against the snow, black as the woman's eyes behind the sights. He heard the hammer click and fleetingly wondered if he would die here, now, at this woman's hands.

He flung himself at her over the last three yards, feeling the heat of the muzzle blast, deafened by the sound of the rifle seemingly discharging right beside his ear.

He sprawled out flat, still short of her, still short. And she was reloading once again . . .

Reflexes controlled Cross now. His reflexes as an animal and his instinct for self-preservation. He snatched his revolver from its holster with a hand that was nearly numb, fumbling it, nearly dropping it, but at last getting the hammer back and the muzzle raised.

The child entered the battle suddenly. Making strange, animal-like sounds in his throat, he stumbled toward Cross, his numbed, frosted hands the only weapons he possessed. The woman cried out something in a thin, terror-stricken voice, called out to try and stop the boy. She raised her carbine hastily, trying to fire before the boy got in the way.

But Cross fired first, and the sound was flat, a bark that was instantly caught up by the wind. The sound of Willow's shot came like an echo, also snatched away, also instantly lost in the howling wind and drifting snow.

She was dead when she fired, and falling, and her bullet caught the boy in the back, slamming him against Cross before he dropped limply into the snow.

Numb and unbelieving, Cross fought his way to his feet. The smoking revolver dropped from his nearly frozen hand.

He stared at the thin, limp, crumpled figure of the boy, lying so still here at his feet. He stared at the young woman, recognizing her as the one they had caught in the Niobrara bottom weeks ago. She was dead, her face like wax, her blood a scarlet stain in the drifting snow. The boy was also dead.

For an instant even the wind was still. Then Cross's tears came like a scalding flood. Great spasms brought them spilling from his eyes. He doubled over and stood there, shaking, choking, making long, shuddering, gasping sounds.

There was no one here to hear. There was only the wind, and the blinding, blowing snow, and this vast emptiness where Willow and the thin, weak boy had come to die.

Morgan Cross wept, standing there. He wept as he had not wept since he had been a child. At last, with no more tears to weep, he turned and stumbled alone through the drifting snow, back toward the White River bluffs and Fort Robinson.

His family had been avenged but there was no satisfaction in him. There was only a sudden, haunting sadness and a terrible, empty sense of loss.